W9-BNJ-313

Also by Henry Cecil

Fiction

FULL CIRCLE

THE PAINSWICK LINE

NO BAIL FOR THE JUDGE

WAYS AND MEANS

NATURAL CAUSES

ACCORDING TO THE EVIDENCE

BROTHERS IN LAW

FRIENDS AT COURT

MUCH IN EVIDENCE

SOBER AS A JUDGE

SETTLED OUT OF COURT

ALIBI FOR A JUDGE

DAUGHTERS IN LAW

UNLAWFUL OCCASIONS

INDEPENDENT WITNESS

PORTRAIT OF A JUDGE

FATHERS IN LAW

THE ASKING PRICE

A WOMAN NAMED ANNE

THE BLACKMAILERS

*

BRIEF TALES FROM THE BENCH

published by the B.B.C.

*

Nonfiction

BRIEF TO COUNSEL

KNOW ABOUT ENGLISH LAW

both illustrated by Edward Ardizzone

NOT SUCH AN ASS

TIPPING THE SCALES

A MATTER OF SPECULATION

(*The Case of Lord Cochrane*)

*

Under the pseudonym of Clifford Maxwell

Fiction

I MARRIED THE GIRL

TELL YOU WHAT I'LL DO

AN INNER SANCTUM MYSTERY

BY

HENRY CECIL

SIMON AND SCHUSTER

NEW YORK

Published in the United States by Simon and Schuster
Rockefeller Center, 630 Fifth Avenue
New York, New York 10020

First U.S. printing

SBN 671-20522-6
Library of Congress Catalog Card Number: 69-15566
Manufactured in the United States of America

CONTENTS

TELL YOU WHAT I'LL DO

1 *With Intent*

There was complete silence in Court One at the Old Bailey. This was not due to some dramatic statement by the judge, counsel or a witness. Nor was it due to the sudden fall from its scabbard of the sword of justice. Some readers may remember that Horatio Bottomley, when he stood in the dock for the last time, threatened the jury with such a fall if they should convict him. On that occasion as on this the sword refused to budge.

But Harry Woodstock, who was in the dock on this occasion, was a far more pleasant character than Horatio Bottomley. It is true that they had certain traits in common. They both liked good living and they both cheated their way through life. But there was nothing sanctimonious or pompous about Harry Woodstock.

His grandfather had been a cheapjack almost straight out of the pages of Dickens.

'Tell you what I'll do,' he'd say. 'I'll add two cups and saucers and sell you the lot for a shilling. What – no takers! You don't know what you're missing. And I'm not going to let you miss it. I shouldn't sleep tonight if I thought you'd missed it. I'd be so upset I'd kick the old woman out of bed, and she weighs sixteen stone. Tell you what I'll do. I'll add the toast racks – that isn't a crack, ma'am – a bit of spit and it's all gone – see? Tell you what I'll do. You can have the lot for a tanner.'

Harry's father did not inherit his own father's criminal instincts. On the contrary, he did quite well in a respectable business and earned sufficient to enable him to give Harry an excellent education. In learning, not in morals. For Harry inherited his grandfather's failing, though he did not consider it a failing. But he did not cheat the small man in the street who could ill afford to lose the pound which Horatio Bottomley had off him without the slightest compunction.

He was an adept at long firm frauds. Many people outside the legal profession do not know what a long firm fraud is. In its simplest form, it means the obtaining of goods upon credit when you have no intention of paying for them, and selling them as soon as possible and making off with the proceeds. There are many varieties of this type of fraud, and if you want to indulge in something a little more sophisticated than the simplest form, there is not much difficulty in arranging it.

Harry got considerable pleasure from this type of fraud. First he used to set himself up in business. This simply meant taking a room at a very low rent, either in one of the provinces, or in London. If he proposed to cheat the people in London, he set up business in the provinces. And if he proposed to cheat the people in the provinces, he set up business in London. He was not particular as to the nature of the business, and he had tried many kinds in his time. He'd been in hardware, software, eatables, drinkables, building materials and so on.

The silence in Court on the occasion of Harry's present trial was due to the nature of the material in which he had been trading. It was toffee. Harry had gone into the toffee business in his normal way. He had rented a small room, called himself The Global Confectionery Company, had good-looking stationery printed, opened an account in a bank, and ordered toffee. His first orders for toffee were always accompanied by a remittance, and a diplomatic letter saying that, as he had only just started his business, he assumed that the suppliers would like to have their money before sending the goods. The suppliers did not object. After paying for several small orders, he asked whether they would now be prepared to give him reasonable credit. Most of them were so prepared. Harry did not at first let them down. At the end of each month he sent a remittance. That is to say, he sent a cheque. And on the first two or three occasions it was always met. Eventually when his credit was sufficiently high, he gave a much larger order to each of his suppliers. On this occasion his cheque was not sent on the due date. When he received polite and then less polite and finally angry threatening letters from his creditors, he sent them each a cheque. And each cheque was dishonoured.

At this stage of the proceedings Harry usually disappeared. And it had certainly been his intention to disappear on this occasion. Indeed he had half disappeared. That is to say, he had given up the room from which he'd conducted his business, and left no forwarding address. But after the police had been informed and were already on his trail – for they soon recognised that it was Harry Woodstock who had been buying the toffee – he suddenly re-appeared and paid all his creditors. To the surprise both of them and of the police, for such a thing had never happened before. It was not playing the game according to the long firm rules. The creditors were, of course, delighted and would have been perfectly prepared to renew business relations with Harry. But the police were not at all delighted. They had taken a lot of pains to trace Harry, they were just about to pounce, and then suddenly by paying up he deprived them completely of the fruits of their work. This was not good enough. A lot of public money had been spent in trying to bring Harry to justice, and Inspector Bream thought that one way or another Harry ought still to be brought to justice. He consulted the department of the Director of Public Prosecutions.

He was advised that, although a prosecution could still be brought against Harry for obtaining goods by false pretences from the various suppliers, since there was evidence that, when he obtained these goods, he did intend to defraud them, it was unlikely that any jury would convict in view of the payment which had been made before he was actually prosecuted. The jury would not know of his previous convictions for similar offences.

But Inspector Bream was not prepared to allow the matter to remain in that unsatisfactory condition. So he proceeded to investigate Harry's sales of toffee. And it was those investigations which led to the present proceedings.

Harry was charged with obtaining money by false pretences with intent to defraud, by falsely pretending that the toffee which he sold to the various purchasers had qualities which in fact it did not have. For good measure, he was also charged with obtaining the goods by fraud from the various suppliers. But the Inspector fully realised that these latter charges might well fail. On the other hand, Harry's failure to pay for the goods in the first instance, his delaying letters and his temporary disappearance would, he hoped, add a flavour to the case which might make it more easy to obtain a conviction on the charge of obtaining money by false pretences on the sale of the toffee.

The silence in court was due to the fact that everyone concerned with the case, except the usher, the clerk and Harry himself, was eating toffee. Harry had submitted to the judge with success that it would not be fair to him if the people who were trying him did not taste the toffee themselves. It was a very sticky toffee, and in consequence neither the judge nor counsel were able to say anything with success.

Harry was at this time in the witness-box with a bag of toffee.

Eventually, the judge managed to say:

'What do you shay thish ish?'

Harry looked at a document in front of him.

'Oh, my lord, I'm sorry,' he said, 'there's been a slight mistake.' He paused.

'What mishtake?' asked the judge.

'I'm terribly sorry, my lord,' said Harry.

'I dare shay you are,' said the judge, 'but whatsh the mishtake?'

'It's a little embarrasshing,' said Harry. 'Oh dear now,' he added, 'I'm sorry, I'm doing it myself. It's a bit catching.'

'Behave yourshelf,' said the judge.

'I'm shorry, my lord,' said Harry. 'Oh dear, there I go again.'

'If I have any more of this nonsensh,' said the judge, succeeding in his first s, but failing miserably in the second, 'I'll remand you in cushtody until you can behave yourshelf.'

The judge was so angry, not only with Harry, but with himself, that he made no attempt to get proper s's in the last two sibilant words.

'I'm very sorry, my lord,' said Harry, 'but it really is rather embarrassing.'

'I don't see why it's embarrasshing to you,' said Harry's counsel who thought he had better take a hand in the affair, 'you haven't got any toffee in your mouth.'

'It isn't that at all,' said Harry. 'His lordship asked me what was in his piece of toffee.'

'Well, tell him,' said Harry's counsel.

'Must I?' said Harry.

'Shertainly,' said the judge.

'Well,' said Harry, and then hesitated.

'Come along, sir,' said the judge, 'I've had enough of this tomfoolery.'

'Well, my lord,' said Harry, 'I'm afraid – I'm afraid – I really didn't mean it, my lord – it was a genuine mistake, my lord' – and then Harry stopped again.

'Out with it, Mr Woodstock,' said his counsel.

'Well,' said Harry, 'I'm afraid I've given his lordship – an – an – aphrodisiac.'

'Rubbish,' said the judge.

'You wait and see,' said Harry quietly.

'What did you say?' said the judge.

'My lord, with respect,' interposed Harry's counsel, 'with the greatest respect, your lordship ought not to say that what my client says is "rubbish" without having the piece of toffee in your mouth analysed.'

'How on earth can I have it analysed now?' said the judge. 'I'm glad to say there's very little in my mouth.'

'Well,' said counsel, 'with the greatest respect, your lordship ought to wait to see if you feel any effects of it before you proclaim to the jury that my client is a liar.'

The judge looked at Harry.

'What did you give to Mr Brent and Mr Hughes?' he asked, referring to counsel on each side.

'Well, my lord,' said Harry, 'I don't know if it was very wrong of me, but I gave counsel for the prosecution, that's Mr Hughes, a depressant, and I gave my own counsel a pep pill.'

'What have the jury had?' asked the judge.

'As a matter of fact,' said Harry, 'I gave them all a soporific.'

The judge thought for a moment, and then addressed counsel.

'Mr Hughes and Mr Brent,' he said, 'it's my fault, I ought never to have allowed this. I apologise. But I suppose we'd better have what's left in Mr Woodstock's bag analysed. What have you got left?' he asked.

'Well, my lord,' said Harry, 'there's another aphrodisiac and the rest are all alcohol of various descriptions. There's one here with Taylor's '48 port. I don't know whether your lordship would like to try that.'

' '48 port with toffee!' said the judge in horror.

'It goes very well, my lord,' said Harry.

'Do you swear,' asked the judge, 'that there is some alcohol in all these pieces of toffee that you have in front of you?'

'Except the one,' said Harry. 'Yes, m'lord.'

'And what do you say is in the one?' asked the judge.

'I may not pronounce it properly,' said Harry, 'but I think it's called cantharides.'

'Well,' said the judge, 'hadn't the case better be adjourned for these pieces of toffee to be analysed?' He looked enquiringly towards counsel, but Harry intervened.

'By all means have them analysed, my lord,' he said, 'but I don't think the analyst will find anything.'

'You mean there's nothing in them for the analyst to find, do you?' asked the judge.

'Nothing that they will find,' said Harry.

'But you've just sworn that there's alcohol in all of them but one.'

'So there is, my lord,' said Harry.

'Then the analyst will find it,' said the judge.

'I don't think so,' said Harry.

'Why not?'

'Because the amount is so small,' said Harry, 'that it will defy analysis.'

'You'd better explain yourself to the jury,' said the judge.

'Tell you what I'll do, members of the jury,' said Harry. 'I'll give you an example. If you put a measure of gin in a gallon jar of water, stir it and take a spoonful of the contents, that spoonful will contain a quantity of gin which any analyst would find. But suppose you took a tablespoonful from that jar and poured the contents into another gallon jar of water, and then took a tablespoonful from that jar and poured the contents into another gallon jar, provided of course the contents were properly stirred, there would be in fact some gin in every jar. But, if you continued the process, it would not be long before the amount of gin defied analysis.'

'Well,' said the judge, 'if there's so little alcohol in each of these pieces of toffee, how do you justify charging extra for them?'

'My lord,' said Harry, 'apart from anything the Prices and Incomes Board may say, surely I am entitled to ask what price I like. There's nothing wrong in asking a high price; they needn't pay it if they don't want to.'

'But,' said the judge, 'people will only pay a higher price if they think they're going to get something additional for their money.'

'They *are* getting something additional,' said Harry.

'But very little,' said the judge.

'I didn't say how much they got,' said Harry. 'I merely said they got some, and so they do.'

'We've only your word for that,' said the judge.

'I'm on oath, my lord,' said Harry.

'A lot of people give evidence upon oath,' said the judge, 'but they don't always tell the truth.'

'That's perjury,' said Harry.

'It is,' said the judge.

'A much worse offence than I'm charged with,' said Harry. 'I think I'm right in saying that perjury strikes at the root of justice.'

'Are you trying to be funny?' said the judge.

'Funny, my lord?' said Harry. 'I'd never do that here, my lord. I have the greatest respect for the courts. I know them well enough.'

'Mr Brent,' said the judge, 'd'you accept that, if an analysis were taken, there would be no sign of alcohol in any of these pieces of toffee?'

'I've no idea,' said Harry's counsel. 'My client doesn't seem to think there'd be any, but he's not a chemist.'

'Then I can see no alternative to an adjournment,' said the judge.

In consequence the case was adjourned so that the pieces of toffee produced by Harry could be analysed. On the adjourned hearing Mr Pomfrey, the analyst, gave evidence.

'This is a high-grade toffee,' he said, 'and it contains nothing but sugar, butter and vanilla.'

'Any alcohol?' asked the judge.

'No.'

'Any aphrodisiac?'

'No. Nothing but toffee,' said the analyst.

Harry's counsel then rose to cross-examine.

'Mr Pomfrey,' he asked as his first question, 'if you took a gallon jar of water and put in a spoonful of gin, stirred it round, and took out a spoonful, that spoonful on analysis would be shown to have some gin in it, would it not?'

'Of course,' said the analyst.

'And if you took out such a spoonful and put it in another gallon jar of water, stirred it round, and took out a spoonful of the mixture, would that be shown to have some gin in it?'

'Yes,' said the witness.

'If you went on with that process,' continued counsel, 'being careful to stir the mixture each time very thoroughly, would it not be true to say that even after ten changes there would be some gin left in a spoonful of the mixture taken after the tenth change?'

'Theoretically, yes,' said the witness.

'By that,' said counsel, 'I take it you mean that you would not be able to discover the amount on analysis?'

'That is correct,' said the witness.

'After how many changes do you think the amount would be undiscoverable?'

'After three, possibly after two.'

'So if after three changes, someone took a syringe and extracted some of the mixture and then inserted some of the contents of the syringe into one of these pieces of toffee, would there not be some amount of gin in that piece of toffee?'

'Theoretically, yes,' said the witness.

'I don't understand what you mean by "theoretically",' said the judge. 'Either there would be or there wouldn't be.'

'I believe,' said the witness, 'there's a maxim in law *de minimis non curat lex*. An amount which defies analysis isn't worth talking about.'

'Well, I'm afraid we've got to talk about it,' said counsel. 'You agree that in the circumstances I have described, there would be some amount, however small, in the piece of toffee?'

'You wouldn't be able to taste it,' said the witness.

'Would it have any effect?' asked the judge.

'None whatsoever,' said the witness.

'Have you ever tried?' asked counsel.

'Tried what?' asked the witness.

'Tried a piece of this toffee with, say, a drug in it, a depressant or a stimulating drug in it in such a small quantity that it could not be discovered on analysis to see what effect, if any, it had on you?'

'I can't say that I have,' said the witness.

'Then,' said counsel, 'how can you be so sure it would have no effect?'

'Well, I am sure,' said the witness.

'Sure of something you've never tested?' asked counsel.

'There's no need to test it, it's obvious,' said the witness.

'Are you not aware,' asked counsel, 'that a good many years ago there was a practitioner who apparently effected cures of deadly diseases by this method?'

'I have read about such a case,' said the witness, 'but I don't agree that he did effect cures. He claimed to have effected them, and some people thought he'd effected them.'

'In that case he prescribed powders for his patients.'

'I believe that was so.'

'And those powders were analysed, and the analyst could only find sugar and substances of that kind.'

'I believe so.'

'No drug of any sort or kind.'

'Quite.'

'And that practitioner swore that in fact those powders contained an infinitesimal amount of a certain drug, did he not?'

'I believe that was the case.'

'He claimed, did he not, that this infinitesimal amount of drug stimulated what he called the "vital force" to repel the disease from which the patient was suffering?'

'Yes, he claimed that.'

'And did not a large number of people, some of them well known, back up his claims to have cured them?'

'That is so.'

'Are you in a position to swear positively that all these people were wrong?'

'All what people?' asked the judge.

'The practitioner and all his patients,' said counsel. 'Is the witness prepared to swear that they were all wrong?'

'How can I swear about that case?' said Mr Pomfrey. 'I doubt if I was born when it arose. So I've had no opportunity of testing anything that was said in it.'

'If what was said in it was true,' said counsel, 'how can you dispute that the same may be true in the present case?'

'I should be very surprised if it was,' said the witness.

'That's another thing altogether,' said counsel. 'Many things are surprising. That is all I wish to ask, my lord.'

That concluded the evidence of Mr Pomfrey, and Harry went back into the witness-box.

'Now, Mr Woodstock,' asked the judge, 'how did you insert this alcohol or this other drug into the pieces of toffee?'

'With a syringe,' said Harry.

'Do you mean to say,' said the judge, 'that you solemnly inserted the syringe in every single piece of toffee which was sent out to the purchasers?'

'Not in all,' said Harry. 'Some of them I sold as a chance lot.'

'What do you mean by a "chance lot"?' asked the judge.

'What I say,' said Harry. 'I said that there was a chance that, if you bought these toffees, one of them would contain whatever it was I said it contained.'

'What were the chances?' asked the judge.

'That depended on the price,' said Harry. 'If you wanted a near-certainty, it cost more. If you were content with a ten to one chance against, it cost less.'

'But,' said the judge, 'it must have taken you hours and hours, however many chance lots you sold.'

'It did take me hours and hours,' said Harry. 'I enjoyed every one of them. It's not work that requires a lot of thought, and I can think about all sorts of things while I'm doing it. Might I ask your lordship a question?' he added.

'Certainly not,' said the judge.

'It's rather important,' said Harry.

'Later on,' said the judge, 'you can speak to your counsel, and he may ask me a question if he wishes, but I don't promise to answer.'

'Can I ask him now?' said Harry.

'Oh, very well,' said the judge. 'Mr Brent, would you mind going over to the witness-box and speaking to your client?'

Counsel went over to the witness-box.

'What is it?' he asked in an undertone.

'Ask him if the toffee has had any effect on him,' said Harry.

'I don't want to be disbarred,' said counsel.

'Well, ask him if it tasted any different,' said Harry; 'there's no harm in that surely. What did yours taste like anyway?'

'If you're not prepared to treat this case seriously,' said Harry's counsel, 'I shall retire from it.'

'I don't see why you should get so excited,' said Harry. 'It's I who stand the chance of going to gaol, not you. If I can be cheerful about it, so should you be.'

Counsel went back to his seat.

'I do not propose to ask your lordship anything,' he said.

Eventually Harry's evidence was concluded, counsel made their speeches and the judge began to sum up.

Among other things, he said this:

'Members of the jury, the accused is charged with various offences. But one group is quite distinct from the other. In the second group of offences he is charged with obtaining goods by false pretences. Put in ordinary language, that means that he cheated the suppliers into sending him goods for which he never intended to pay. Well, counsel has said on his behalf, quite correctly, that he has in fact paid for them. Although you may think his behaviour, after he'd ordered the goods and in the first instance failed to pay for them, rather suspicious, counsel submits that it is very difficult for you to be sure that he intended to cheat the suppliers when in fact he has not cheated them, and they've all been paid in full. You may think there's a great deal in that submission.

'The other group of charges relate to his supplying the toffee to the purchasers. There it is said that he made pretences about the toffee which have been proved to be untrue. That by those pretences he induced the purchasers to pay more than they would otherwise have been willing to pay. It is said by the prosecution that this toffee can be obtained from various sources, and that it would be absurd to imagine that purchasers would pay a higher price to Mr Woodstock than they would pay to other people unless he said something to induce them to do that. And what he did say was that the toffee that he sold them had various qualities which the toffee supplied by other distributors of toffee did not possess. You heard the evidence of Mr Pomfrey that none of these pieces of toffee contains anything except the normal ingredients of toffee. You heard Mr Woodstock say that in fact he inserted an infinitesimal quantity of various alcohols or drugs into many of the pieces of toffee. You also heard Mr Pomfrey admit that there was a case where a practitioner of medicine – not a qualified practitioner – purported to have cured people by giving them a similarly infinitesimal quantity of a drug. Whether in fact he did cure them, we shall never know. The question which you have to decide in the first instance is, was any quantity of any drug or any alcohol inserted in any of this toffee? If you are satisfied beyond all reasonable doubt that it was not, and if you're satisfied that the purchasers would not have bought this toffee but for the representation that it had this additional quality, and if you're further satisfied that Mr Woodstock made this false representation in order to cheat those who bought the toffee from him, then you will be satisfied that the case for the Crown has been proved. But unless you are fully satisfied on all these matters – and I repeat that it is for the Crown to prove them, and not for Mr Woodstock to disprove them – unless you are fully satisfied on all these matters, the accused is entitled to be acquitted.'

The judge looked at the clock.

'I will finish my summing up after lunch,' he said, and rose.

Fortunately for Mr Woodstock, the judge did not notice that from the dock he was being offered another piece of toffee.

Harry was taken down to the cells during lunch. A kindly prison officer had brought him an early edition of the evening paper, and he read it with interest. Then he saw something in the stop press which made him swallow his last mouthful whole.

Meantime the judge was having his lunch.

'I see you've got Harry Woodstock in front of you,' said the recorder.

'A friend of yours?' asked the judge.

'Not exactly,' said the recorder, 'but a nice fellow. I've had him in front of me twice. I gave him three years the last time. Long firm fraud. I can't help liking the fellow, he's so cheerful about it all. What are you trying him for, the same?'

'Yes and no,' said the judge. 'He's certainly got some long firm charges against him, but they're not going to stick. Because he's paid up.'

'Paid up?' said the recorder in a surprised tone.

'Yes,' said the judge.

'Where did he get the money from?' asked the recorder.

'I don't exactly know,' said the judge. 'The important thing is that he paid, and I can't see any jury convicting him of those charges. Indeed, I shall suggest that they don't.'

'What's the other charge?' asked the recorder.

The judge told him. 'He may very well get off that

too,' he added. 'I shall give the jury every chance to acquit him.'

'I hope they do,' said the recorder.

After lunch the judge came back into the court and was starting to resume his summing-up when Harry rose in the dock.

'My lord,' he said.

'Silence,' said the usher.

'My lord,' repeated Harry.

'What is it?' said the judge. 'You shouldn't interrupt.'

'I want to change my plea to "guilty",' said Harry.

'What!' said the judge.

'Guilty,' said Harry.

'Have you spoken to your counsel about it?' said the judge.

'I haven't had the chance,' said Harry.

'Well, you'd better do so. I'll rise to give you the opportunity.'

The judge rose and Harry's counsel went to see him down below.

'What is all this?' he asked.

'I want to plead guilty,' said Harry.

'But why? You've got a jolly good chance of getting off,' said his counsel.

'Well, I am guilty,' said Harry.

'You told me you weren't before,' said his counsel.

'I dare say I did, but repentance never comes too late, does it?'

'Do you want to plead guilty to all the charges, or only some of them?'

'All of them,' said Harry.

'But you're almost bound to get off one lot.'

'Not if I plead guilty,' said Harry.

'But were you guilty of those too?'

'What d'you think?' said Harry.

'It doesn't matter what I think.'

'That's all right, then,' said Harry. 'I want to plead guilty, and that's all there is to it.'

'You'll get four years, you know.'

'Naturally,' said Harry.

'I think I must have this in writing,' said Harry's counsel.

'You can have it by deed if you like,' said Harry.

'But why are you doing this?' asked his counsel.

'Because I've seen the light,' said Harry. 'I'm very ashamed of myself. Taking up all your time, all the time of the judge and the jury and so on. It's disgraceful of me.'

'Well, I don't understand it at all,' said Harry's counsel.

'You don't go to church, that's your trouble,' said Harry. 'There is more joy in heaven over one sinner that repenteth than over ninety and nine just men.'

'I do go to church as a matter of fact,' said Harry's counsel, 'but I don't believe you've repented. There's some other reason for this.'

'What possible reason could there be?' said Harry.

'I've no idea. But there is one.'

'That's not very charitable of you,' said Harry. 'If you go to church you should know that charity is one of the important things in life. Can't you believe that for once in my life I'm sorry, and want to do the right thing?'

'I could believe it,' said counsel, 'but I don't.'

'Well, that's got nothing to do with it,' said Harry, 'has it? It doesn't matter what you believe. I ask you to tell the judge I want to change my plea. You've got to do it, haven't you?'

'Yes,' said Harry's counsel, 'if you're really serious, I have. But I shall have it in writing, please. I'll get my solicitor to give you a document to sign.'

Harry duly signed the document, and, when the judge came back, Harry's counsel said to the judge:

'My lord, after careful consideration my client informs me that he wishes to change his plea from "not guilty" to "guilty".'

'Very well,' said the judge. 'On what charges?'

'On all the charges,' said counsel.

'On *all* the charges?' queried the judge.

'Yes, my lord,' said counsel.

'No doubt you have advised your client, Mr Brent?' said the judge.

'Of course, my lord. He says he fully understands and wishes to plead guilty.'

'Very well then,' said the judge. Harry was duly asked if he wished to change his pleas of 'not guilty' to 'guilty' on all the charges, and he said he did.

'Members of the jury,' said the judge. 'As the accused has been placed in your charge, you have to give a verdict upon the matter. You have now heard the accused say that he is guilty of all the charges, and presumably you will therefore return a verdict that he is so guilty.'

'Do you wish to say anything in mitigation?' the judge asked Harry's counsel, after the jury had convicted him and evidence of his previous convictions had been given.

'Yes, my lord,' said counsel, 'I do.'

'No, my lord,' said Harry, 'he doesn't. I've wasted a lot of your lordship's and the jury's time already, I don't want to waste any more. I am guilty, and that's the end of the matter.'

'As my client apparently doesn't want me to say anything,' said Harry's counsel, 'I won't.' And he sat down.

'Harry Woodstock,' said the judge, 'you have now pleaded guilty to a large number of charges, most of which are of a similar kind to those of which you've been previously convicted on seven occasions. I don't know whether your sudden determination to plead guilty indicates a change of heart, and a desire to go straight when you've served your sentence, but I can only say that I hope that that is the case. But you've been committing this sort of crime for years, and it's obvious that a fairly substantial sentence must be passed. You have already served sentences varying from three years downwards. They do not seem to have had any good effect upon you. Whether a longer sentence will have any good effect upon you or not, I cannot tell. But it will be for others and not for me to see if you can in some way be reformed. My duty is to pass upon you a sentence of five years' imprisonment.'

2 *Albany I*

A little over three years later Harry was in Albany, Isle of Wight. Albany is in one respect the latest disgrace in English prisons. It is a new prison but unlike its celebrated namesake in Piccadilly, it has no proper lavatories for the people for whom it was built, the prisoners. The disgusting slopping-out system still continues there. The Home Office and each successive Government appear to be determined that those who are convicted of crime shall not merely be punished, but degraded. In spite of expense and security problems some other countries have managed to do away with the system, and it may legitimately be asked why it is continued in the latest English prison.

Twice in 1968, Lord Gardiner, the Lord Chancellor, said that he would like to see the old prisons blown up. 'That is all they are fit for,' he said. In fact some of these prisons could be sold at a profit by the Home Office to property developers. They could probably be sold for a sum which would enable the Government, at no expense whatever to the country, to build a decent prison somewhere else. But that can't be done, said the Lord Chancellor, because of a Prison Act passed nearly a hundred years ago. It is quite true that under that Act, if the prisons were sold, with the law as it is at present, the proceeds, or the bulk of them, would have to go to the local authorities concerned. But these authorities cannot be expected to have relied upon the value of the prisons in balancing their accounts. In these circumstances it would be no injustice to the local authorities if what a Victorian parliament gave to them, an Elizabethan parliament should take away. A bill for this purpose should have the support of all parties and, if it did, it could soon become law. The prisons then could swiftly be sold and swiftly come down. And Lord Gardiner's wish would be fulfilled. If, therefore, the Government and the Home Office really want to improve the situation in the prisons, it is difficult to understand why they raise the old Act as an insuperable obstacle.

Unfortunately prison reform is not valuable from the party political point of view. The public at large does not much care what happens to prisoners inside prisons so long as they are not beaten up. And the continuation of the slopping-out system in Albany coupled with the failure to introduce the necessary legislation to get rid of the old prisons suggests that there is insufficient enlightenment among those in authority.

Harry was not unhappy in prison. He was in fact seldom unhappy. The only thing that made him unhappy was violence, or the thought of it. He hated the idea of being hurt. He had served throughout the 1939–45 war in fear and trembling. And in fear and trembling he had saved his colonel's life. It was a curious coincidence that, while Harry was weathering the storm in Albany, I.O.W., his colonel was enjoying the delights of Flat Q in Albany, Piccadilly.

Harry had been his batman, and the colonel had kept in touch with him after the war. Harry had no difficulty in deceiving his previous master into thinking that he had done very well in the business world. Accordingly, when he went away for twelve months, eighteen months, three years, and so on, he was travelling on the continent or in America or somewhere else.

at almost the end of the case, you changed your plea, and said you were guilty. I must say I had hoped that that showed that you too had made the great discovery.'

'I'd made a discovery all right,' said Harry, 'but not the same as yours.'

'Why did you change your plea, then?'

'You think it was a sign of true repentance, don't you?' said Harry.

'I couldn't think what else it could be,' said the canon.

'Well, I hate to disillusion you,' said Harry, 'but at any rate, it's the truth.'

'What's the truth?' asked the canon.

'I suddenly decided that I would be happier in prison.'

'I can't believe that,' said the canon. 'You like high living, I know that, and there's nothing wrong in it, within reason. You certainly don't get high living here.'

'And yet,' said Harry, 'I'm happier here than I would be outside. And that's the truth.'

The canon was silent for a short time. He was thinking hard. How could Harry be happier in prison, unless the outside world had become too much for him? That must be the answer. It was not at all surprising. Most recidivist criminals were of low mentality. They went in and out of prison almost automatically, and they hardly thought about it at all. They hardly could think about it. But Harry was quite different. He was intelligent, had a sense of humour, and was obviously capable of enjoying himself considerably. It must either be that the struggle to lead an honest life was too hard for him, or that the continual fear of capture must be too great a strain. Many people have a temptation to throw themselves off the side of a cliff or in front of an oncoming train, not because they're tired of life, not because they have any particular troubles, but simply from fear. The fear is that they may fall over, and they could end it by throwing themselves over, thus releasing themselves forever from that fear. That is what Harry must have done when he changed his plea to guilty.

'I believe I understand,' said the canon, 'and I'm sure I can help you.'

'I hate to say it,' said Harry, 'but you don't understand. You like doing good, and I like doing bad.'

'It can't have been bad to change your plea to guilty,' said the canon. 'That at any rate was the truth. And nothing bad ever came out of the truth.'

'I can't agree about that,' said Harry. 'The truth is often quite useful, sometimes essential, and sometimes absolutely wrong. D'you tell the truth to a dying man who does not want to know that he is dying? D'you dash the hopes of his relatives by telling them that there is *no* hope?'

'Such decisions are hard, I agree,' said the canon, 'but in the end I am sure that the truth does more good than harm. In the case you mention, it prepares the doomed man and his relatives for what is going to happen. They can face it better when their knowledge is sure. Uncertainty makes for greater anxiety than certainty.'

'D'you never tell your wife that she looks lovely when she doesn't?' asked Harry.

'Never,' said the canon. 'And that makes her even happier when I am able to tell her with conviction that she does look lovely. And that I'm glad to say is often. In the short term I grant you that a lie often seems more expedient. But that doesn't mean that it's right. It was no doubt expedient for you to plead not guilty and try to persuade the jury to acquit you. But it was not right, and I believe that you eventually realised that. That's why you changed your plea. There's a lot of good in you, Harry, whatever you say.'

'Well, you've got to believe that,' said Harry, 'it's part of your religion. We are all sinners, but God is in all of us.'

'I wish you believed that,' said the canon.

'I do sometimes,' said Harry.

'But why are you happier here than you would be outside?' said the canon. 'If it's really true that you're happier.'

'It's safe here,' said Harry.

'I think perhaps I understand. You mean there are no temptations here? You can't do wrong because there are no opportunities?'

'Well, that's one way of putting it,' said Harry, 'but it's not the right one.'

'What are you going to do when you get out?' asked the canon. 'Why don't you start a legitimate business for once?'

'It would feel all wrong,' said Harry. 'Fancy paying for goods you'd bought on credit.'

'Come now,' said the canon, 'that won't do. When you start off on one of your long firm businesses, you always begin by paying for the goods.'

'That's true,' said Harry, 'but they're only very small orders. It's extraordinary how people fall for it. I buy half a hundredweight for cash, and then they send me five tons on credit.'

'How long is it before you're found out?' said the canon.

'Oh, it varies,' said Harry. 'Sometimes I've never been found out at all. Or perhaps it would be more accurate to say I've never been found. It's not all that easy to find one person out of fifty million. I give the police full credit for finding me at all.'

'They know you too well by now.'

'That's true,' said Harry. 'I must find a new trademark.'

'So the truth is,' said the canon, 'you don't really want to earn an honest living?'

'The truth is,' said Harry, 'I don't want to *earn* anything. If I could just sit back and receive, I'd be fine.' He paused for a moment. 'But I'm not sure that I would, though; I'd miss the fun. You've no idea what a kick I get out of some of the letters from my creditors. The first one, venturing to think that I may not have received their original account, and enclosing with it their very best wishes. The second one, asking me if I would be kind enough to settle their account. The third one, saying that this account is really now very much overdue, and they must request an immediate settlement. And so on and so forth. And there are so many varieties of them. And then my letters are quite fun too. Sometimes I send a cheque and forget to sign it. Sometimes I put a year ahead or a year behind. Sometimes I put one thing in the figures, and another in the words. Oh yes, there's plenty of variety.'

'Have you never thought,' said the canon, 'that many of these people whom you cheat are decent fellows – I was going to say like yourself – husbands, fathers of children and so on, and some of them are quite small people who can't afford to lose the money?'

'Oh no,' said Harry. 'They're very seldom small people. If they are, it's a mistake on my part. Small people have to be much more careful than big ones. Have I ever told you about the blotting-paper lark?'

'I don't think so,' said the canon.

'You can only do that,' said Harry, 'with a really big firm. A firm where they issue cheques for large sums and very large numbers of them. You go along with some really good blotting-paper and you see the manager or at any rate you see somebody who has got power to give you an order. They are usually in a bit of a hurry. They want some blotting-paper, and your blotting-paper is really good blotting-paper. So you persuade them to give you an order. You make out an order form and get them to sign it. The figure on your form is ten, and they think it's for ten boxes or something of that sort. In fact it's for ten dozen gross boxes. Enough blotting-paper to last them for about ten years. In due course you render an account, and the wretched man who sees the account suddenly finds what a bloomer he's made. Either he's got to admit to his superior what he's done, or to put in a cheque along with the rest of them, and hope it will pass unnoticed. Ten to one it will. Now I leave it at that because I'm not greedy, but there's another ploy which some people use. A couple of years later they call back, and if the chap's still there, they ask him to sign another order.

' "But I've got all the blotting-paper we want for years and years," he says.

' "Does your boss know about it?"

' "What's that got to do with you?"

' "Unless you sign another order, he will."

'What's the poor fellow to do?' said Harry. 'Either he's got to admit to the chap immediately above him, first of all that he gave an order which he ought never to have given, and secondly, that he put a cheque through for the full amount without telling them what had happened. He'd get the sack for that. So he signs another order, and pushes another cheque through, and ten to one that goes through all right. By this time his firm have got enough blotting-paper to last until the end of the century. Well, I wouldn't do the second part of that. Too much like blackmail.'

'It is blackmail,' said the canon.

'No violence and no blackmail,' said Harry. 'Those are my rules, and I stick to them. Just honest to God fraud. Most people are dishonest one way or another, the only difference between me and them is I admit it.'

'It might surprise you to know,' said the canon, 'how many

people are not dishonest at all. And most of those who are dishonest are only dishonest in small ways.'

'I once heard a judge say,' said Harry, 'that he never cared for the defence that it was only a little one.'

'Well, it's better than a big one,' said the canon.

'Look at the things people do to avoid paying income tax and surtax,' said Harry.

'Most of them are within the law,' said the canon.

'Are they moral just because they are within the law?' asked Harry.

'No,' said the canon, 'some of them are not moral, and I wouldn't do them myself.'

'What's the worst thing you've ever done?' said Harry.

'I'm not prepared to tell you,' said the canon.

'I wouldn't know the worst thing I'd ever done,' said Harry, 'but I don't know that I'm all that bad. I only cheat people, I only tell lies. Politicians do the same. Even Sir Stafford Cripps said that, if necessary, he'd have told a lie to the public. To the public, mark you, not just to half a dozen people like I do, but to the whole British public. A Chancellor of the Exchequer. Then they make promises which they don't keep. I break the law all right, but I'm not sure that there aren't plenty of others who never break the law but are much worse than I am morally.'

'Many prisoners say that,' said the canon. 'But it's no excuse for them or for you, even though it's true. Now I must be going. If there is anything I can do to help you when you get out, you know you've only got to ask. Where will you be staying?'

'In Albany, to begin with,' said Harry.

'No, I mean when you come out,' said the canon.

'That's right, the other Albany.'

'You haven't got a flat *there*?'

'Good gracious no,' said Harry, 'they wouldn't have the likes of me. No, I've got a friend there. My ex-C.O., as a matter of fact. I've a standing invitation to go there whenever I want, so it's a good place to kick off from. And the name being the same, I won't feel so homesick.'

'Good,' said the canon, 'now I really must be going.'

He shook hands with Harry and turned to go. And as he did so, was surprised and pained to receive a heavy blow on his jaw from Harry, the man who hated violence.

3 Canon and Convict

A prison officer arrived shortly afterwards, and the net result of Harry's surprising behaviour was that he lost 80 days remission. It is less surprising that the canon, although he was a compassionate man, and ready to forgive, did not visit Harry for some little time afterwards. But he eventually called to see him again, though he did ask first whether Harry wanted to see *him*.

'I'm terribly sorry,' said Harry on their first meeting.

'I just don't understand,' said the canon.

'I shall have to explain,' said Harry. 'I don't want to, but it's only fair to do so.'

'But what a hypocrite you are,' said the canon. 'You pretend to dislike violence, and then you land me a horrid blow on the chin. It was most painful. It continued to hurt me for quite a week or ten days.'

'I am sorry,' said Harry, 'I hated doing it. But I couldn't think of any other way.'

'Any other way of what?' said the canon.

'Any other way of losing remission,' said Harry. 'If I'd hit a prison officer, he might very well have hit me back before he reported the incident. It's a very legitimate way they have of discouraging violence against themselves. He would have hit me very much harder than I could hit him.'

'I see,' said the canon, 'you *wanted* to stay in prison?'

'Exactly,' said Harry. 'You will remember you referred on that occasion to the fact that I wasn't going to lose remission. I had committed a number of prison offences quite deliberately in order to lose it. And, when you told me that in spite of them I should be released in a fortnight, I had to think of some method of avoiding release which would not involve personal violence to myself. And I had to think quickly.'

'I see,' said the canon, 'it's only violence *to* yourself that you object to, not violence *by* yourself.'

'No,' said Harry, 'though I don't blame you for saying that. I don't like violence at all. If I could have thought of some other certain means of losing remission, I'd have taken it. But you were going, and I couldn't think of anything else. Except, of course, of hitting a prison officer. But I hope you won't blame me for not doing that. If somebody had to suffer, it was much better that you should. Some of the prison officers are very good fellows, one of them especially, but if somebody's got to be hurt, it's always better that it should be a Christian. That avoids the possibility of revenge.'

'Well, it's quite true,' said the canon. 'I had no wish to hit you back.'

'You see,' said Harry, 'I knew I was right. I hope you've forgiven me,' he added.

'Yes, of course,' said the canon. 'But I should like to know why you want to stay in prison.'

'I told you last time,' said Harry, 'it's safer.'

'D'you want to spend your life here?' said the canon.

'Not if I can help it,' said Harry.

'Then there's something special you're frightened of outside prison?'

'Yes,' said Harry, 'there is.'

'Is that why you pleaded guilty?' asked the canon. 'In order to get into prison?'

'You're getting warm,' said Harry. 'Indeed you're there. That is why.'

'But you fought the case to begin with, so I was told. Why did you suddenly change your mind? Did you suddenly learn of something?'

'That's right,' said Harry. 'I suddenly learned of something. In the stop press in the evening newspaper. I learned that a man had escaped from prison.'

'Someone you're frightened of?'

'Very much so,' said Harry.

'D'you know him well?'

'I've only met him twice,' said Harry.

'Why does he hate you so much?'

'He doesn't,' said Harry. 'Not yet anyway.'

'Well, I can't make you tell me,' said the canon, 'but you may feel that it's only reasonable to tell me in the circumstances. As you know, everything you say is entirely confidential.'

'All right, I'll tell you. This chap was the leader of that bank robbery where they got away with a hundred thousand pounds. I'd met him in prison, and just before the police closed in on him, he handed me sixty thousand pounds to keep for him. They caught him a couple of days later, but he escaped while I was being tried.'

'You've spent the money, I suppose?' said the canon.

'Not all of it,' said Harry. 'I've got enough left to get started up again when I come out. And this man will be after me from the moment I leave the prison, and he'll kill me when he finds that I can't hand over to him the bulk of what he gave me. Or if he doesn't kill me, he'll leave me unrecognisable. I can't bear the thought of it, and the only place I'm safe is here.'

'Why don't you hand the money you've got left over to the bank, or to the police?' asked the canon.

'He'd kill me just the same,' said Harry. 'More so. If I keep the twenty thousand pounds and give it to him, that would be something.'

'But it's not your money,' said the canon, 'it's the bank's.'

'Another bank's got it now,' said Harry. 'It doesn't make all that difference. Anyway they've amalgamated now. It was stolen from the National Provincial, and I've put it in the Westminster. That's fair enough, isn't it?'

'You mean it's in your name in the Westminster?'

'It's in a name I use,' said Harry. 'The banks aren't all that keen on opening accounts for people who've got previous convictions.'

'But how d'you know the man's in England?'

'I don't. He may not be. But he will be as soon as he hears I'm out. What would you do in my position? You'd want to hide, wouldn't you?'

'Well, it's difficult to imagine myself in your position,' said the canon. 'I haven't any previous convictions, you see.'

'Let's assume I hadn't,' said Harry. 'Supposing a chap comes up to you and says: "Here's the proceeds of a robbery, sixty thousand pounds, keep it for me until I come out, chum."?'

'Well, that's simple, I'd have just taken it to the police.'

'Well, they'd have been a canon short,' said Harry, 'when he caught up with you.'

'No doubt I'd get police protection until he was caught again. You could get police protection if you handed in the money you've got left.'

'I've got police protection now,' said Harry, 'the best I can get. Once I get out, they're not going to spare half a dozen men looking after me for the rest of my life. They've got better things to do. I'm not worth it, I don't pretend I am. Well, what would you do if you were me?'

'If I were you,' said the canon, 'presumably I'd do what

you would do. You're asking me what I would do if I were in a similar position.'

'Well, put it another way,' said Harry. 'What d'you advise me to do?'

'Well, that's simple. I advise you to give up the money that you've got to the police or the bank, and to ask them to protect you.'

'If I took your advice, how would you feel when you read of my being murdered?'

'I'd be very sorry,' said the canon. 'But I'd still feel I'd given the right advice.'

'Oh, it's the obvious advice,' said Harry, 'I grant you that. It's the school solution and all that. Indeed, what else could you say? You know I've got money which doesn't belong to me. You're bound to tell me to give it back. It's the correct legal advice, it's the correct moral advice. Indeed, it's everything except the right advice,' said Harry. 'As far as I'm concerned, it's a death sentence, or possibly something worse. I don't want to be maimed for life. And then on top of it, they'd probably charge me with receiving money knowing it to have been stolen.'

'They might do a bargain with you,' said the canon doubtfully.

'A bargain over forty thousand pounds!' said Harry. 'Can you hear the Commissioner of Police saying: "All right, my boy, you spent forty thousand pounds belonging to the bank, you shouldn't have done that, it's naughty. But in view of your admirable record, we'll let bygones be bygones, and we'll give you protection for the rest of your life, provided you hand over what you've got left." That sounds likely, doesn't it?'

'Receiving stolen money is almost worse than stealing it,' said the canon.

'What did I tell you?' said Harry. 'That's what the Commissioner would say. If there were no receivers, there would be no thieves. But, to tell you the truth, I didn't want this money. I couldn't help taking it. He came to me in a great hurry, and said: "You know what to do with this. God help you if you spend a penny of it." I wish I'd said to him what I thought – that God helps those who help themselves – then he wouldn't have left it with me.'

'Well, if you wish you hadn't got what's left,' said the canon, 'why don't you hand it over?'

'Hand it over to whom?' said Harry. 'The police or the bank? Not likely. At least I'll have something to give to him when he comes along.'

'But it's not his money.'

'Of course it isn't,' said Harry, 'but that's not the point. It's my life and my body. I haven't got much of a chance as it is. Think of it from his point of view. It took a lot of time and trouble and nerve to work out that bank raid. Two or three months' work, maybe, and then they might have been unlucky. And he would certainly get twenty or thirty years if he was caught.'

'How much did he get?' asked the canon.

'Thirty.'

'But he got away after one.'

'But he must be hopping mad that he hasn't got the money with him. He'll have been a long time without it. That's enough to make a man feel violent. If I ever felt violent, it would make me feel violent.'

'So you didn't feel violent when you knocked me down?' said the canon.

'Certainly not,' said Harry, 'I hated every moment of it. That's true. But I'd rather hit you than have someone else hit me.'

'Well,' said the canon, 'what are you going to do when you come out? You've got to come out some time, you know, even if you knocked me down again now. They might charge you, I suppose, with an extra offence and sentence you for that, but it's unlikely. And so when your time has expired, you'll have to go. They won't let you stay. You can't book a room here.'

'All I can do,' said Harry, 'is to get back here as quickly as possible, and I hope you'll come and see me. It helps to pass the time. But I'll be worried stiff until I do get back here, I can tell you. You don't know these chaps, you've only read about them. I have seen them. If you'd seen that chap's face when he said: "God help you if you touch a penny of it", you'd have known that he meant it. Do you think God will help me, by the way? You should be in his confidence.'

'Well, I'm not.'

'Well, more than I am,' said Harry.

'But I tell you something,' said the canon. 'This may surprise you, but I think you're worth helping. I think that in spite of everything you've done, and everything you're going to do, I still believe in you.'

'But I couldn't go straight if I tried,' said Harry, 'and I don't want to try.'

'That's what you say now,' said the canon. 'Why don't you get married? That would give you something to stay out of gaol for.'

'As a matter of fact that's why I haven't got married. I'd hate to think of the wife and kids outside.'

'Would you have married if you hadn't taken to this life?' asked the canon.

'Oh good lord, yes,' said Harry. 'I'm very fond of women. I find a different one every time I come out.'

'Why never the same?' said the canon.

'I've just told you,' said Harry, 'I might marry her, and that wouldn't be fair.'

'Well, you've got some decent feelings anyway,' said the canon.

'Of course I have,' said Harry, 'I'm full of decent feelings. It just happens that I won't conform.'

'If you married, you'd have to,' said the canon.

'Precisely.'

'If you say you change your woman every time you come out, that means you like variety,' said the canon.

'Yes,' said Harry, 'perfectly true.'

'You want variety in life?'

'That's it,' said Harry.

'You've had half a lifetime of crime, why don't you vary it by having the other half as a respectable married man?'

'Well,' said Harry, 'first of all it wouldn't be all that easy to find somebody to marry me unless I told them a lot of lies, and you wouldn't approve of that, would you?'

'No,' said the canon, 'I wouldn't.'

'But why not?' said Harry. 'Suppose it's true that, if I got married and had a family, I'd reform and become a respectable member of society, that would be a good thing from everybody's point of view, wouldn't it?'

'Of course it would.'

'Supposing I could only get married if I told lies to the girl, wouldn't the end justify the means?'

'The end never justifies the means,' said the canon, 'if the means are a lie. In the end only truth will prevail. From the practical point of view your wife would eventually find out who you were, and she might leave you in consequence.'

'Not if I'd chosen the right girl,' said Harry. 'Women are like that. They stick to you, whatever you've done, if they really love you. But do you think I'm justified in having children?' asked Harry. 'Apart from the fact that I might transmit some of my less fortunate qualities to my children, would it be fair to have children when their father has been to prison as often as I have? "What's your father do?" "Well, at the moment he's doing five years." Would that be fair to a child? You can ask a girl if she's prepared to take you on with all your previous convictions, but you can't ask your children if they're prepared to let you beget them. Tell me, if I told you that I'd go straight for the rest of my life on getting married, would you advise me to let some poor girl get herself tied up to me?'

'If she knew the truth and was prepared to accept it, yes,' said the canon.

'Well, I think it would be a shocking thing to do,' said Harry, 'truth or no truth.'

'What exactly then do you propose to do when you're thrown out of here?'

'Well, as I told you, I shall go and plant myself on my ex-colonel. Then I shall find a nice young woman with whom to spend the next few weeks. And then I shall have to do something rather different. And it will take a bit of working out.'

'What d'you mean by that?'

'Well, I've got to get back to prison as quickly as possible. On the other hand, supposing my bank robber friend should in the meantime be caught, I want to have an escape route so that I shan't be convicted. You're right in thinking that I prefer the life outside, provided I can live it in safety. In reasonable safety, that is. Nobody's safe today. If you're not killed on the road or by a block of flats falling down, you are just as likely to be invaded by one of the viruses or germs which have been released by the cure of other illnesses. Nature certainly has a sense of humour, or perhaps it's just obstinacy. But, as fast as the doctors are able to pronounce that a particular deadly disease can be cured, nature provides another one to do the job. And if it thinks it isn't doing the job fast enough, it arranges a war. You've got to keep the population down, haven't you?'

'Cynicism is no answer,' said the canon.

'I don't pretend it is,' said Harry, 'but it's a remarkably effective defence. I'm frightened of violence, as you know. But, suppose I spent my time worrying about what the scientists could do to us with nuclear and biological warfare and I don't know what else, life wouldn't be worth living. As a matter of fact, I find life well worth living, even here. I don't pretend I like it here, but I can make my plans for the future in complete security. I don't even risk being run over, and I'm certainly not going to become overweight on the rich prison food. Prison undoubtedly reduces the chances of a coronary. And it's much cheaper than those palaces in the country where they give you nothing to eat and charge a fantastic amount for it. As a matter of fact, it would be a wonderful prescription for doctors to give to their less wealthy patients. Six months in prison would do a lot of people a lot of good.'

'In their present crowded state,' said the canon, 'I doubt whether the authorities would accept a prescription, even from the most highly qualified doctor.'

'Oh, he wouldn't be able to do it directly,' said Harry, 'but he could do it just the same.'

'How d'you mean?'

'It's quite simple. "I recommend a course of shoplifting," the doctor will say on his prescription. The first time you'll only be fined £2, say, or bound over. Next time the fine will go up a bit. After you've done it half a dozen or more times, they'll have to send you to prison. Of course it will take a little time, but not all that much if the prescription is a good one. "It is very important," it will read, "that a dose should be taken every day except Sundays, when the shops aren't open." I should think one could pretty well guarantee to get a person into prison within, say, three months. If you were really clever about it, in less time than that.'

'Mightn't the doctors be charged themselves with inciting people to commit crime?'

'I hadn't thought of that,' said Harry. 'As a matter of fact it would probably do them good too. The number of doctors who suffer from the same complaints as they are trying to heal is quite significant. I know that a girl friend of mine who suffers from asthma went to a big consultant to get some treatment, and he started to treat her. And then on one occasion she was informed by his secretary that she was sorry the doctor was ill. "I'm very sorry," said my friend, "I hope it's nothing serious." "Oh no, just asthma," said the secretary.'

'So you'll go to Albany, Piccadilly,' said the canon, 'you'll find a girl friend, and then what?'

'Perhaps you can give me an idea or two,' said Harry. 'I've got to make sufficient evidence against myself to ensure that I'll be charged with an offence, and at the same time have a complete defence to the charge, supposing there's no need for me to go to gaol after all. Any suggestions?'

'I shouldn't think you need any,' said the canon. 'Your brain works far faster than mine when it comes to considering criminal possibilities.'

'It's quite interesting really,' said Harry, 'I've never done this before. As I told you, I've never got tired of the old long firm game because you can ring the changes and deal in different kinds of goods and so on. There's plenty of variety if you look for it. This is quite different. It takes quite a bit of time to get a long firm job going. This has got to be something simple. All the best things are simple. All the best plans are simple. And, if I may say so, all the best sermons.'

'We can agree about that,' said the canon.

'Assault is no good, because the fellow might hit back.'

'How about trying another parson?' said the canon.

'He might be a muscular Christian and hit back harder than ever.'

'Well, a bishop?'

'They're younger than they used to be, and he might have been a boxer.'

'Shoplifting?' queried the canon, and then suddenly thought. 'Good gracious, I oughtn't to have said that; please forget it.'

'It's nice to think you're human,' said Harry. 'Thanks for the tip. Shoplifting's certainly nice and simple. But what about the defence? I'll have to think that one out. Or have you any suggestions?'

'Will you be serious for a moment?' said the canon.

'I am serious,' said Harry.

'Yes, I know,' said the canon. 'That's why I want to have another go at you.'

'Fire ahead,' said Harry. 'I owe it to you really.'

'Now, you're fond of people, aren't you?' said the canon.

'I'm fond of some people,' said Harry.

'But you like people in general. You like your fellow men. You want them to be happy?'

'I don't mind,' said Harry, 'if they'll let me be happy too.'

'Why do you always pretend to be so selfish? Have you never in your life done anything for anybody else?'

'Well, I've had to sometimes,' conceded Harry. 'Couldn't avoid it. But it went against the grain.'

'Wouldn't you help a blind person across the street?'

'That's ridiculous,' said Harry. 'Everybody does that.'

'Or give up your seat on the underground to an older man?'

'I never have one,' said Harry.

'But if a friend came to you for help, you'd give it to him if you could?'

'It depends how much he wanted.'

'Suppose it wasn't money. Suppose he wanted comfort and advice?'

'He wouldn't come to me for that.'

'Oh yes, he might,' said the canon. 'Suppose I came to you and wanted comfort and advice?'

'Well, that's different,' said Harry. 'I've been giving you that for the last few years. I shouldn't mind going on.'

'You think I'm visiting you for my own benefit?' said the canon.

'Of course you are,' said Harry. 'Everyone who visits a prisoner, except a relation or friend, comes for his own benefit. The intelligent ones like you know this. The stupid ones kid themselves into thinking that they're only coming to help the poor prisoners. I'm not saying they don't help them. They often do. But that isn't why they come. Of course the worst of them – there are not many of these – the worst of them come because they get a thrill from coming into prison. It's like going to the zoo, but more exciting.'

'Is that why I come?' said the canon.

'Oh, good gracious no,' said Harry. 'You're one of the intelligent ones. And anyway you've been so often it couldn't give you a thrill any more. No, you've got a mission in life, that's why you come. And I'm jolly glad you have. It's made all the difference to me, if that's any comfort to you. That would be one reason for not seeing you out of prison.'

'Why?' asked the canon.

'If I don't see you out of prison, it would give me something to look forward to when I knew I was coming back. If I can see you just as much out of prison as in, I might as well stay out as far as you're concerned.'

'You'd have made a wonderful lawyer,' said the canon.

'Intelligence coupled with instinct takes you a very long way in that profession.'

'Too late now,' said Harry. 'They wouldn't take me as a student with all my convictions. I could give them a few lectures though. Tell me,' he went on, 'd'you think it's right that if I really wanted to go straight all respectable professions would be barred to me now because of my past?'

'I don't see any alternative,' said the canon, 'because how could they know for certain that you would be going straight?'

'They couldn't,' said Harry, 'and the chances are I wouldn't be.'

'You could be of the most tremendous use in the world if you wanted to be,' said the canon. 'Let's assume for the moment that you want to stick to crime, and that nothing will change you.'

'All right.'

'There are a lot of your fellow prisoners who don't want to stick to crime, who'd give anything to be out of it. To be back in the world. To be respected. To be able to live a normal, happy life, like other unconvicted people. You could help them.'

'I'm glad you said "unconvicted",' said Harry, 'not "respectable".'

'Most unconvicted people are respectable,' said the canon.

'What d'you mean by respectable?' said Harry.

'They conform,' said the canon.

'Oh that,' said Harry. 'Most of them are too frightened not to. Take judges for example. They're no better than other people, morally I mean. There are lots of things they'd like to do – and would do too – if they weren't frightened for their own position. As for sinning in their hearts, I suspect they sin a good deal more there than most people because they daren't sin in fact. The same applies to all people in prominent positions. People either conform because they haven't got the guts not to or because they're frightened not to.'

'Are there really no good people in the world at all then?'

'Of course there are,' said Harry, 'but you're talking about the population at large. You're talking about getting criminals back into society. This beautiful society which conforms. All of whom love their neighbours as themselves, I don't think!'

'Many of them do,' said the canon.

'So long as they're not competing together,' said Harry. 'Look at them on the road. Watch them drawn up at traffic lights, then they love their neighbours as themselves all right. "How are you, old boy! What's the time, old boy? Rotten weather, old boy! D'you know how far it is to so-and-so, old boy?" and so on. But watch these old boys as soon as the cars start off. It's one mad rush to get in front of the other. D'you think it would make any difference if every car had a placard on it: "Love your neighbour as yourself"?'

'It ought to,' said the canon.

'It shouldn't need a placard,' said Harry. 'But these people you want me to bring back into society, you've met them of course?'

'A good many, yes.'

'Well, how many are capable of it? Now, I am sorry for some of those chaps. They've never had a chance, and never will. There's nothing I could do for them, they've no will, no spirit.'

'They were born with both,' said the canon.

'Very little of either, I'm afraid,' said Harry. 'And what little they had they soon lost. Most of them come from broken homes or institutions, and the bulk of them haven't even got the guts to have a grievance. You should know. You must have tried often enough. Had some of them to stay with you, I don't doubt. All they do is pinch the spoons.'

'Not all of them,' said the canon.

'Have you had any success with a real old lag?' asked Harry. 'A chap who's been in and out of gaol for years. Who as often as not can't read or write. Whose intelligence quotient is a minus quantity.'

'Some of them are fond of animals and children.'

'Oh and women too,' said Harry. 'That I grant you. They've got instincts. Instincts of the human animal, pat a dog, give sweets to a child, and you know what to a woman. Have you had any single proved success?'

'I think so,' said the canon, 'though I admit I can't be absolutely sure. But if you're sorry for them, why won't you help? You could, you know. Because you speak their language, and you speak our language too. You're the perfect person to act as a go-between. Why won't you help?'

'Believe it or not,' said Harry, 'I have. I gave a thousand pounds to the Discharged Prisoners Aid Society.' He paused. 'I didn't, as a matter of fact, but I really thought of doing it.'

'From the bank money, I suppose,' said the canon.

'Of course,' said Harry. 'I couldn't afford to give my own, could I? I tell you what, I'll give it to you, if you like, and you can use it to help people.'

'The thousand pounds, you mean?'

'Two thousand, if you like. I'm getting sentimental.'

'Sentimental with the bank's money.'

'It's all very well for you to call it the bank's money,' said Harry, 'but I'm going to use it for myself. Either as a sop to throw to the man to whom it really belongs—'

The canon interrupted. 'To whom it really belongs?' he said.

'You know what I mean,' said Harry. 'The man who's got a better claim to it than I have, shall we say. Either I'm going to keep it for that or use it myself. If I give some of it to you, I shan't have it for either purpose. That's unselfish, isn't it?

That's almost as good as giving away my own money. Look, I'll make it three thousand.'

'You'll offer me the whole lot before you've finished,' said the canon, 'because you'll be quite sure that I won't take it. Would you offer me any if you thought I'd take it?'

'Oh yes,' said Harry, 'I'd offer you something. But of course I might never give it to you. At any rate you know you can't trust me an inch. You can't believe a word I say. If I make a promise, I'll only keep it if it's to my own advantage. But I'll pat a dog, I'll give sweets to a child, etc. etc.'

'Talking of et ceteras,' said the canon, 'how do you set about finding your young woman?'

'That's easy,' said Harry. 'You've no idea what a lot of nice young women there are. And in the most unlikely places. And you're right, kindness will go a long way with them, and that's the card I play. And they respond to kindness like flowers to the sun. That's why I don't keep any one of them too long. They'd want to marry me, and I might get sentimental one night and do it next morning. Or two mornings after. I think you've got to wait forty-eight hours or something like that. Would you marry us?'

'I'd be very pleased,' said the canon.

'Well, you ought to be ashamed of yourself.'

'I won't say that kindness is all,' said the canon, 'but it's going a very long way indeed. And whether you like it or not, you are a kind man. You can't help it. I dare say you were born that way. But that's how it is.'

'Well, I'll have to put up with it, then, won't I?' said Harry. 'But you have to tell lies to be kind sometimes, don't you?'

'It's quite true,' said the canon, 'that people do sometimes tell lies thinking that they're being kind. I don't dispute that sometimes truth is departed from for reasons which are believed to be good. All I say is that they are not good. The truth must never be tampered with. But that doesn't mean to say that people who tell lies with a good object are bad people. I quite agree with you, often they're not. They're merely wrong-headed.'

'Tell me,' said Harry, 'which d'you think is the better, a kind thief, or an unkind man who conforms to the rules?'

'A kind thief any day,' said the canon. 'You don't have to labour the point to me that a lot of people who keep to the rules are far worse than people who don't keep to them. But society has to have rules, and when they're broken, it has to take action about them. Will you do me a favour, Harry?' he asked.

'I doubt it,' said Harry. 'But tell me what it is.'

'Will you try going straight for, say, two months when you come out?'

'Good gracious, no,' said Harry, 'I've got to get back as quick as I can.'

'Suppose they catch the man?'

'Then I shall have to reorientate myself,' said Harry. 'But if I went straight, what am I to live on? Would you call it going straight if I lived on the money I've saved out of the bank robbery?'

'You could send the money to the police anonymously,' said the canon.

'And how would I start up again then?'

'I told you I could get you a job.'

'I don't want a job,' said Harry. 'I like business. Buying and selling and so forth, and preferably not paying for what I've bought.'

'Well, I shan't give up,' said the canon.

'Neither shall I,' said Harry.

4 *Albany II*

Harry arrived at Albany, Piccadilly, just as the colonel was going out.

'My dear boy,' said the colonel, 'why on earth didn't you wire or telephone?'

'I would have, sir,' said Harry, 'but I didn't get the chance. I was in New York and didn't expect to be coming back for several weeks, and then suddenly I had a telephone call which made me have to catch the next plane back. So here I am.'

'Well, it's good to see you, my boy,' said the colonel. 'Come in and have a drink.'

'But you were just going out.'

'That can wait. Why, it's years since I've seen you. Where have you been?'

'All over the place, sir,' said Harry. 'Australia, New Zealand, America, Japan, oh and I don't know where else.'

'Everything going well, I take it?' said the colonel.

'Couldn't be better,' said Harry.

'I'm glad of that,' said the colonel, 'because there's a little business matter I'd like to talk to you about. You won't mind?'

'Not at all,' said Harry.

They went back into the colonel's rooms, and the colonel gave Harry a drink and took one himself.

'Well, here's fun,' said the colonel.

'Here's luck, sir,' said Harry.

'I've unexpectedly been left a sum of ten thousand pounds,' said the colonel, 'and I'm wondering what to do with it. Nothing seems safe these days. I hope you don't mind my asking, and I'll quite understand if it's impossible, but I suppose you haven't got room for it in one of your businesses?'

'I'm terribly sorry, sir,' said Harry, 'but one thing we're not short of is money. That's all we have got really. In terms of goods, factories etc. What we lack is human material. Young men and women with brain and brawn. You need brawn these days. Flying across the Atlantic every other week takes it out of you, you know. You lose five hours sleep one way.'

'I hope you don't mind my mentioning it,' said the colonel.

'Not at all,' said Harry, 'and I'd love to take it off you if I could. It goes against the grain, refusing ten thousand pounds. But really I wouldn't know what to do with it. I'd have to put it on deposit at a bank, and you can do that just as well as we can. There's no shortage of money in this country if you've got a sound business.'

'I wish I'd asked you about it five years ago,' said the colonel. 'I might have changed some of my own investments then. But still, I mustn't grumble, I manage. But it's wonderful to think of you who were only a batman in the war now in a position to buy me up several times over. What beats me is why you never wanted to become an officer.'

'To tell you the truth, sir,' said Harry, 'I'm not officer material. I'm not a leader of men. I can organise money and goods, but not men. Well, men come into it, of course, but to be an officer in a war you've got in effect to be able to lead your men in the charge on a beautiful white horse. Well, I can't ride anyway, and, if I could, I'd want to lead them like the Duke of Plaza Toro from the rear.'

'You didn't behave like that when you saved my life,' said the colonel.

'Hang it, sir,' said Harry, 'you were paying me five shillings a week as your batman, it was the least I could do.'

'I'm sure it was seven and six,' said the colonel. 'How long are you in London for?'

'Two or three weeks, I expect,' said Harry.

'Well, stay here, of course.'

'It's very good of you, sir.'

'Nonsense. I shouldn't be here at all if it weren't for you. Now what about your luggage?'

'Well, as a matter of fact,' said Harry, 'I came away in such a hurry I've practically got nothing with me.'

Without a word, the colonel got up and led Harry into the bedroom.

'You see that wardrobe,' he said; 'it's full of my clothes. Wear them. We're about the same size. I don't say they're as good a cut as your own, but they come from Savile Row. See that chest of drawers,' he said, 'full of shirts and underclothes, they're all yours. Wear them. That's an order.'

'Sir,' said Harry.

'And make yourself free of this flat. The drink and everything else in it.'

'Sir,' said Harry.

'And if you want to bring a friend to stay, bring him.'

'Sir,' said Harry.

'I'll tell the porter so that he'll know who you are,' said the colonel. 'Let me see.' He stopped for a moment or two and ran his hands through his hair. 'My God,' he said at last, 'it's old age. D'you know I can't remember your name. That's a nice thing. Forgotten the name of the man who saved my life. But forgive me, old man, I'd forget my own name for two pins. It's Woodthorpe or something, I know it is. No, it's not Woodthorpe. Now, what is it? Don't tell me. Woodbridge. No, that won't do. Bridgestock, Birdwood. Am I close?'

'Well, yes and no, sir,' said Harry. 'Because, as a matter of fact, I've changed my name. A distant relative left me some money on condition that I changed it. I never understand why people do these things. After all, a few thousand pounds free of tax is not to be despised.'

'I don't suppose it means much to you fellows,' said the colonel.

'Oh, I don't know,' said Harry, 'it's remarkable how little we've got over, after we've paid all the taxes and things.'

'Well, more than seven and six a week, I should think,' said the colonel.

'Yes, a bit more,' conceded Harry. 'I've got rather an odd name now, as a matter of fact. It's Princewig.'

'Good gracious,' said the colonel, 'then I must have known the fellow. He died about a couple of years ago. He lived in Northumberland. There can't be two Princewigs in the country. I was at school with his aunt.'

'His aunt?' queried Harry.

'Yes. Prep school, you know. Boys and girls of that age are all the same thing. Different a few years later. Are you married?'

'No,' said Harry. 'But I've got expectations.'

'Splendid,' said the colonel. 'Take an example from me. Who'd want to be a crusty old bachelor? I'm all three. I'm crusty, I'm old, and I'm a bachelor. No good to anyone. You know this is about the first civil word I've spoken for a fortnight. I bite everyone's head off. Just like it used to be in the old days. Remember?'

Harry remembered. 'You weren't as bad as all that, sir,' he said.

'I was shocking,' said the colonel. 'The sort of chap who causes a ruddy red revolution. I'm surprised you didn't cut my throat sometimes. Instead of which you kept me alive. I can't think why. The trouble is I enjoy it. I'd bite a man's head off soon as look at him. Not so easy in peacetime. D'you know what? I go into a shop and I treat everyone as though they were in my battalion, on orders. And they don't like it. I don't actually tell them to stand to attention, but near enough. "Would you mind not scratching yourself while you're talking to me," I said to one man. "I'm not going to be spoken to like that, even by a customer," he said. "I'm not a customer," I said, and walked out. How they must have hated me in the battalion. I hope so anyway, I love being hated.'

'Well, I'm sorry to disappoint you, sir,' said Harry, 'they loved you. Every man of them. The more you swore at them, the better they liked it. I remember old Emery, the cook, at battalion headquarters, saying: "He's a bit of an old so-and-so, but my God, he's a soldier." '

'Yes,' said the colonel meditatively, 'I suppose there was a place for me in wartime. I made my company commanders so angry that they went into battle swearing. They couldn't take it out of me, so they had to take it out of the Germans, and by Jove they did. D'you remember my pep talk just before Alamein? I can almost repeat it to a word. "We're going into battle," I said. "If it weren't for the men under you they'd knock us for six. I've met some scruffy officers in my time, but of all the scruffiest of the scruffy, you take the prize. You're a lazy lot of good-for-nothing scroungers. You wouldn't be fit to be a lance-corporal in peacetime. It's lucky that in this war officers are not supposed to be gentlemen. None of you would qualify if they were. Now I'll tell you the plan." Then I gave them their orders. At the end of it: "I don't suppose you've understood a word," I said. "Any questions?" One of them spoke up. Good chap he was, I forget his name. No, I remember, it was Halliday. That's right, Halliday. "Colonel," he asked, "what is your actual reason for insulting us before each battle?" "I'll tell you," I said. "I don't suppose we shall meet again, and I wanted you to know what I thought of you. Good luck," I added. They were a good lot of chaps on the whole, but they needed a war to put any fight into them. I put in Halliday for a V.C. after it was all over. Posthumously, I'm afraid. How they must have hated me.'

'They didn't really,' said Harry.

'Then I was a failure,' said the colonel. 'There are two ways of setting about commanding men. One of them is the way Monty did it. Very successful I grant you. He was the best general of the lot. The other way is my own pet invention. Make them hate you, and they take it out on the other side. The trouble is it doesn't work in peacetime. I've got so into the habit I can't help it. I repeat, you're the first person I've spoken a civil word to for a fortnight. The servants here can't stand me. I treat them like dirt, and tipping well doesn't make up for it. They've got pride, these chaps.'

At that moment the telephone rang.

'Excuse me,' said the colonel. He lifted the receiver.

'Hello,' he said. 'No, I don't.' And he slammed down the receiver. 'There,' he said, 'that sort of thing doesn't make a man popular. Now I'm going off for a week. I've got another key.' He opened a drawer and got out a key and gave it to Harry. 'Here it is. Don't go before I come back. It's a change to be polite to someone, it does me good. But God help the next man I meet, he'll be for it.' And the colonel strode out of the room leaving Harry in possession.

First of all he had a good look round the flat. Then he helped himself to a drink, and went and inspected the colonel's wardrobe. He selected some good-looking clothes, took off his own, and put the others on. Then he went out and strolled to Bond Street. He went into one of the big jewellers where even the commissionaire breathed wealth. Everything was soft. The carpets were soft, the voices were soft, and, of course, the women.

'Can I help you, sir?'

'I'd like to see the manager,' said Harry.

'I'm afraid the manager's out at the moment, but I'm in charge. Is there anything I can do?'

'Well, there is, I suppose,' said Harry. 'My name is Stout. Harry Stout. At the moment I'm staying in Q5 Albany. I'm about to get engaged to a young lady, but I'm not sure if she knows it.'

'Quite so, sir,' said the assistant deferentially.

'I want to give her a really stunning piece of jewellery. Something really expensive. I don't mind if it's a bracelet or a ring or a necklace or what it is, so long as it's expensive, and expensive-looking. It must be something that has "genuine" written all over it.'

'All our genuine articles have that, sir.'

'Have you any, then, that are not genuine?'

'When I say genuine, sir, I mean all our expensive articles. There's no doubt about any of them. You can't fake a diamond or an emerald or a ruby. About how much did you want to spend, sir?'

'I'm not particular,' said Harry. 'Anything from two to five thousand pounds.'

'Will you come this way, please, sir.'

Softly they went into a special office which was reserved for customers who were spending a lot of money. Softly Harry was invited to sit down on a soft chair. After he'd waited a few minutes the assistant returned and proceeded to show Harry his wares.

'How much is that necklace?' he asked.

'Three thousand five hundred pounds,' said the assistant.

'I'd like something a bit better,' said Harry.

Meanwhile the assistant had looked Harry up and down several times to try and decide what manner of man he was. There were so many thieves and confidence tricksters about, one could not be too careful when dealing with high-priced jewellery.

'Forgive my asking, sir,' he said, 'but will you be paying cash for this?'

'I'll be giving you a cheque, if that's what you mean,' said Harry.

'Quite so,' said the assistant.

There was a pause during which Harry added:

'I realise of course that, as you don't know me, you'll want to be sure about the cheque. I'll give you the name of the bank, and you can telephone the manager and ask him if the cheque is good for the money.'

'That's very good of you, sir,' said the assistant. 'It's just a formality, of course.'

Formality my foot, thought Harry. He gave them the name and address of his bank.

'You're welcome to ask them,' he said, 'if a cheque for five thousand pounds drawn by me would be met. Perhaps you'd better get the manager on the telephone, and I'll speak to him so that he can recognise my voice. I've already told him that I was coming to you or to somebody else.'

'Thank you, sir. I'll look up the number.'

'I have it,' said Harry, and he gave the assistant the number.

A few minutes later the manager confirmed that Harry's cheque for £5,000 or even more would be duly met. As Harry had £10,000 in a current account, and £10,000 on deposit with that bank, the answer was not altogether surprising. Eventually Harry chose two pieces of jewellery. One a bracelet and the other a necklace. One was £4,500, and the other £4,700.

'I imagine,' said Harry, 'that a piece of jewellery like this is pretty well known in the trade?'

'How d'you mean, sir?'

'You don't sell a piece like this every day, do you?'

'By no means.'

'And surely jewellery is very much like pictures. For example, Wildensteins will know if the Marlborough Galleries have got a particular Monet. So presumably you know if Cartiers have got something special which I might prefer to this and vice versa.'

'I see what you mean, sir,' said the assistant. 'With the very important pieces, that would be the case. But I hope you're not going to go elsewhere.'

'I hope not too,' said Harry, 'but it depends on the young lady.'

'You want to bring her to see them, of course?'

'No,' said Harry, 'I want you to bring them to me for her to see. Could you or one of your assistants bring them round after lunch one day to Albany?'

'With pleasure, sir.'

'Good. Then that's all, thank you very much. I'll give you a ring and tell you when I'm ready. I've got to find the young lady first, haven't I?'

Harry left the shop and then set about finding the young lady. It took him five days. Sonia Evesham seemed to fill the bill pretty well. She was a half-trained secretary, good-looking, cheerful, and she seemed to like Harry.

It was not long before Harry had installed her in Albany. It is true that the colonel had implied that he could bring any man friend to stay, but Harry assumed that the masculine included the feminine, as in most Acts of Parliament. After they had got to know each other reasonably well Harry explained his plan. Then he telephoned the jewellers and asked them to send a representative with the jewellery in question. Half an hour later the man arrived.

'But they're lovely,' said Sonia. 'You're much too good to me.'

'No,' said Harry, 'I'm not too good to anybody. Good, if you like. But not too good. Which do you prefer?'

Already instructed, Sonia chose the more expensive one. Harry wrote out a cheque.

'Just leave it as it is, please,' he said. 'I'm very grateful for all the trouble you've taken.'

The man expressed the hope that they would be seeing Harry again, and Harry said that it was extremely probable that they would.

'Please thank your manager or assistant manager very much for all you've done for me.'

The assistant went away.

'Now, you're not going to get me involved,' said Sonia.

'Of course not,' said Harry. 'It's nothing to do with you. I merely wanted you there to make the story sound a bit more plausible. Strictly speaking I needn't have had anybody. But now I must get down to business. Excuse me.'

Harry went to the telephone and dialled the number of his bank and asked to speak to the manager.

'It's Harry Stout speaking,' he said. 'I've just issued a cheque to some people,' and he named the jewellers, 'for a bracelet I bought from them. But I think there's a flaw in it, so will you kindly stop the cheque.'

The manager agreed and a stop was immediately placed on the cheque.

'Now here's £20 for you to go and amuse yourself with,' said Harry to Sonia. 'I may not be back for a little time. In fact it's just possible I won't be back until tomorrow. But make yourself at home. The colonel won't be back for a couple of days.'

Harry then went off to a jewellers' shop near to the place where he'd bought the bracelet.

'D'you buy jewellery?' he asked.

'Of course,' said the assistant.

'What'll you give me for this?' He produced the bracelet.

The man was a little taken aback.

'That's a very valuable bracelet,' he said.

'I shouldn't want to sell it if it weren't,' said Harry. 'What'll you give me?'

'Forgive me a moment,' said the assistant. He left Harry at the counter.

A minute or two later a much older man came forward.

'Good afternoon, sir,' he said. 'I understand you want to sell this piece.' And he looked at the bracelet on the counter.

'That's right,' said Harry. 'How much?'

'As this is a very valuable piece,' said the man, 'and I'm afraid we don't know you, sir, might I ask its antecedents?'

'Certainly,' said Harry. 'I bought it just opposite.'

'How long ago, might I ask?'

'Quite recently,' said Harry.

'Might I know why you didn't take it back to them?' asked the man.

'I didn't choose to,' said Harry. 'I preferred to go somewhere else. I might get more from you.'

'Very unlikely,' said the man.

'Well anyway, how much will you give?' said Harry.

'I must take some advice about this,' said the man. 'Please forgive me.' He went out.

Harry sat down and waited patiently at the counter.

In the meantime the jewellers, where Harry had bought the

bracelet, had discovered to their horror that the cheque had been stopped. But, before they could telephone Harry at Albany or go round there, a telephone call was made to them by the jewellers where Harry was waiting.

'This is a police matter,' they both said, and one of them rang up Scotland Yard.

Half an hour later a detective-inspector from the C.I.D. arrived, Harry was invited to come into the manager's private office, and he did so.

'What is your name, please, sir?' asked the detective-inspector.

'Why d'you ask?' said Harry.

'I'm investigating a complaint made by the jewellers who sold you this piece of jewellery that you've given them a cheque in respect of it which has been dishonoured. And within ten minutes of its dishonour, here you are trying to sell it to somebody else. Don't you think that in the circumstances it is reasonable to ask what your name is?'

'Most reasonable,' said Harry. 'Well, I've several names, but your department will know me best under the name of Harry Woodstock.'

'D'you care to give any explanation of your conduct?' asked the detective-inspector.

'Not at present,' said Harry, 'but I haven't committed any crime.'

'But can you explain how it is that you're trying to sell a piece of jewellery for which you haven't paid? And indeed in respect of which you've given a dishonoured cheque?'

'It sounds bad, put like that,' said Harry. 'But I've got a perfectly good explanation.'

'That's what I'm asking you for,' said the detective-inspector.

'I don't see why I should give it at the moment,' said Harry.

'Where are you staying?' asked the detective-inspector.

'In Albany,' said Harry. 'Piccadilly, you know, not Isle of Wight.'

'Well, Mr Woodstock,' said the detective-inspector, 'I could take you into custody on a charge of stealing this by a trick. But, if I'm satisfied you're really living in an apartment at Albany, I'll probably issue a summons for obtaining it by false pretences.'

'That's very civil of you,' said Harry. 'I'd very much prefer a summons. I don't at the moment want to be arrested. It would mean getting bail. And, though I usually do get bail, it's all rather a nuisance. So, if you'd like to come back with me to Albany, the porter will identify me and you can see that I really am staying there. Incidentally, the jewellers where I bought this came round and saw me there. You can enquire from them.'

'I will,' said the detective-inspector.

In consequence of the enquiries made by the detective-inspector, Harry was eventually summoned for obtaining the bracelet by false pretences with intent to defraud. By this time Sonia had departed, and the colonel had returned. Harry arranged to receive the summons personally at the police station, so as to avoid the embarrassment of the colonel learning about it. After he'd received the summons, he lunched with the colonel at his club.

'It's good to see you again, Harry,' the colonel said over their first drink. 'I've had the most unmentionable time. I hate staying in other people's houses, but I've got to sometimes. But I confess I'm not very popular when I do because I always tell the truth. My hostess asked me if my morning tea was all right. "It may have been," I said. "I only had one sip. I seem to remember telling you I didn't like sugar in it. It was like golden syrup. I poured it down the sink." The next morning

I was asked if the tea was better. "What was in the cup was delicious," I said; "most of it was in the saucer." "Have you slept well?" they asked me. "Abominably," I said. "I'm terribly sorry," said my hostess, "I wonder what it was." "It was the bed," I said. "It's one of the most uncomfortable beds in which I've ever slept." "Oh, I *am* sorry, we'll have it changed," she said. The next morning: "Was that any better?" "Not in the least," I said, "and the windows are so small you hardly get any air through." "We'll change your room, then," and so they did. The next morning: "How was it this time?" she asked. "Not a wink," I said. "Your infernal central heating makes noises as though there are alligators in the pipes." I have to go to these people because they get hurt if I say "no". I can't think why. They hate it as much as I do when I come. Still it came to an end at last, but not before I'd had to complain about the hot water. "It was stone cold," I said; "well, a little bit was tepid to begin with, but then it ran cold." "I'm terribly sorry," said my hostess, "I can't think how it happened." "It's happened for seven days," I said. "You don't mind my telling you, I hope, but I'm thinking of the next guest. He may not be so good-tempered as I am, but if you've had no sleep at night, and then are offered a stone-cold bath, it makes you a bit grizzly." "Well, I'll try and lay on an especially good dinner to make up," she said. "I hope you like the claret," my host said later, "it's something rather special. Would you like to guess what it is?" "You wouldn't like the answer if I did," I said. "D'you really want to know what I think of it?" My host threw his hand in. "No," he said, "I don't. Have some barley water instead." I accepted with alacrity and having tasted it I said: " '07, I suppose?" '

'Well, I'm sorry you had such a bad time, sir,' said Harry.

'I'm glad,' said the colonel. 'It made me angrier than ever. You should have heard me talking to the ticket inspector on the train. "What d'you want to see my ticket for?" I asked. "Don't you believe I've got one? If you think I'm travelling first with a second class ticket, I can tell you I'm not. I bought the ticket, paid the full price, which is much too much, and I want to be left in peace. That's why I chose an empty carriage." "I'm sorry, sir," said the inspector, "I have my duty to do." "Well, come back in half an hour," I said. "I'm sorry, sir, I must see it now." "Well, it's going to take some time," I said. "You've a right to see it under your byelaws, I suppose?" "Yes, sir," he said. "Do your byelaws say how long a passenger is allowed to take before producing the ticket?" "No, sir." "All right; well, it's going to take me half an hour," I said. "If you'd like to sit down, do. Or, as I said before, you can come back in half an hour." "You're being extremely awkward, sir," he said. "Of course I am," I said. "I intend to be awkward. Your trains are often late. Sometimes they don't go at all. Sometimes they are dirty. That's awkward for the passengers. Now it's my turn to be awkward." "Might I have your name, sir?" he asked. "Certainly not," I said. "You've no right to my name unless I've not got a ticket, and I tell you I have got a ticket, and I'll show it to you, in my own good time." "You're not taking it out of British Railways, sir, you're taking it out of me," he said. "That's the best I can do," I said. "If you'll show me how to take it out of British Railways, I'll do that instead." As a matter of fact he was quite a good chap, that inspector. I couldn't make him angry whatever I did. I count that as one of my failures. I've never told you about my worst failure, have I?'

'I don't know, sir,' said Harry.

'No, I haven't, I always intended not to. But it's such a long time ago now, perhaps I will. I put you in for a D.C.M., and you never even got a mention.'

'That was very good of you, sir,' said Harry.

'Good of me, rubbish. You earned it. It was that damned brigade major. I couldn't stand his guts, and he couldn't stand mine. The result was I never got anything I wanted from brigade. Nothing. I'd only to ask for something for them to tell me I couldn't have it. And what riled me more than anything was his oily way. He had a greasy smile which I could see even if I was only on the telephone. I remember once I started to say: "You tell the brigadier from me——" "Yes, sir," he said in his oily way, "I have my pencil ready to take down your message for the brigadier." Now what could I say? I had to end it up lamely. Of course I could bite the brigade major, but that didn't do me any good because the brigadier always stood behind him. If I'd said to him, as I'd often wanted to: "Major, take that oily grin off your face", he'd have had the brigadier on my back in no time. I was nearly bowler-hatted as it was. But I'm sorry about you, Harry, you deserved it. They might at least have given you a Military Medal. But not even a mention. I ask you. Now, tell me about yourself. What have you been doing? Made another million pounds while I was away?'

'Not quite,' said Harry, 'only a few thousand.'

'Wonderful,' said the colonel. 'And you were my batman, I often think of it. I hope you're going to stay quite a long time this time.'

'I'm afraid not,' said Harry. 'I shall be off pretty soon I expect. It was awfully good of you to let me stay.'

'Stuff and rubbish, man,' said the colonel. 'Don't you ever say that to me again. You're always thanking me. It's for me to thank you, but I can't go on doing it every minute. It's little enough I've done for you anyway. A couple of suits and a bed, what's that? By the way, was that your secretary who came in this morning?'

'Yes, sir,' said Harry.

'Pretty girl. But all you tycoons can get as many as you like, I suppose. When are you off, then?'

'I should think in about a fortnight,' said Harry, who had not yet been committed for trial, but who expected it to happen the next day.

'I'll come and see you off,' said the colonel.

'Oh, you mustn't bother,' said Harry. 'Anyway I'll probably leave in the middle of the night.'

'I don't care. It will do me good.'

'As a matter of fact,' said Harry, 'it's all rather hush-hush. I shouldn't tell you really, but I do a bit on the side for the Secret Service.'

'Good gracious,' said the colonel, 'that explains your being my batman. Now I understand. That's why you were such a tough guy.'

'No one's supposed to know that I'm going off, sir, so you'll understand if I prefer not to be seen off?'

'Of course, my dear boy,' said the colonel, 'I quite understand. No one can say you waste your time. It's about time you had a break. What you need is two or three months in the country with nothing to do.'

'As a matter of fact,' said Harry, 'I may be able to get that shortly.'

'Well, let me know where you are, and I'll come and see you.'

'Actually,' said Harry, 'there's a sort of hide-out where we all go, and the only thing against it is that we mustn't have visitors. But it's a wonderful rest, I enjoy every moment of it.'

5 *Canon and Colonel*

A fortnight later Harry's case came up at the Old Bailey. There was no news of the bank robber and so, when called upon to plead, he pleaded guilty.

'Are you sure you want to plead guilty?' asked the judge.

'Yes, my lord,' said Harry.

'As you're not represented, I think I'd better go into the matter a little bit more. D'you mind if I ask you some questions?'

'Yes, my lord,' said Harry.

'It's in your own interest,' said the judge.

'Thank you very much, my lord, I am most grateful. But I know my own mind. I'm guilty and I plead guilty.'

'But,' said the judge, 'from the enquiries which the police made, it's plain that you had the money to pay for this jewellery.'

'I stopped the cheque, didn't I?' said Harry.

'Yes, I know,' said the judge, 'but you offered the piece for sale to the jeweller opposite the place where you'd obtained it. I simply don't understand.'

'It's quite simple, my lord,' said Harry. 'I obtained these goods on credit, because, if you give a cheque which isn't met, it's the same as obtaining goods on credit, and I tried to sell them for cash without any intention of paying for them.'

'Well, if you say so,' said the judge, 'there's nothing I can do about it. But I hope you realise that the sentence for a serious crime like this must be a long one, particularly in view of your record.'

'Don't make it longer than you can help, my lord,' said Harry.

'I strongly suspect,' said the judge, 'that, if you'd chosen to plead not guilty, you'd have been acquitted of this charge. Then you wouldn't have had any sentence at all. Are you sure you don't want to change your mind?'

'Quite sure, thank you, my lord,' said Harry.

'Very well then,' said the judge. 'In view of your record I must treat this case seriously. But, as I've said before, it's a very odd case, and I don't believe I know the whole truth about it. Possibly you're covering up for somebody else, but, if that's the case, people who cover up for other criminals must learn that it's not going to pay them to do so. However, in spite of your record, in view of the fact that nobody has lost anything as a result of your behaviour, you will go to prison for three years.'

'Thank you, my lord,' said Harry.

In due course he arrived back at Albany. The reason why Harry was normally sent to Albany, a maximum security prison, was not because he was an escaper himself, but because it was known that he could and did arrange escapes for other prisoners on suitable terms. At Albany, even Harry's plans could not be utilized successfully.

One of the first people to greet him was the prison officer who, according to Harry, was rather a decent chap.

'Well, you haven't wasted much time,' said the officer.

'I couldn't wait to get back,' said Harry.

'You're an odd chap,' said the officer. 'You really seem to like it here.'

'I make the best of everything,' said Harry. 'If I'm in a

hotel where the food's bad and the service worse, I don't grumble. I accept it. After all I might have been in prison. And, when I'm here, I remember that I'm not paying for it, and I might have been in a hotel where the food was bad and the service worse. There's nothing wrong with the service here.'

'I'm glad you think so. What about the food?'

'Keeps my weight down,' said Harry.

'What d'you do in civvy street?' asked the officer.

'Nothing,' said Harry. 'That's why I always get back here.'

'I can't make you out,' said the officer. 'You're not like most of the dopes we've got here. Doesn't freedom mean anything to you?'

'Oh yes,' said Harry, 'freedom means everything. But for the moment I've got all the freedom I want here.'

'Have you ever been examined by a doctor?' asked the officer.

'Often,' said Harry. 'But not for my head. That's all right.'

'Well,' said the officer, 'if you want any help when you go out, I could probably arrange for it.'

'That's very good of you,' said Harry, 'I'll remember.'

A few days later he received a call from the canon.

'I made it, you see,' said Harry. 'But only just. The judge nearly refused to let me plead guilty. Shows I'd got my escape route worked out pretty well, doesn't it?'

'Pity you didn't have to use it,' said the canon.

'You can say that again,' said Harry.

'You seem more anxious to get out this time than last time,' said the canon.

'I met a nice little girl,' said Harry, 'and I would have liked a few more weeks with her. Not long enough to get to the marrying stage.'

'What does your bank think of it all?' asked the canon.

'Very starchy,' said Harry. 'They asked me to take my money away. Can you beat it? That must have hurt them. Twenty thousand pounds, they don't like turning that away, but they did.'

'What have you done with it?'

'Put it in a safe deposit.'

'How was your colonel?'

'Oh, full of life. He wanted to invest £10,000 with me.'

'And you wouldn't take it?'

'I couldn't very well,' said Harry.

'Why not?'

'Oh, I just couldn't.'

'Slipping, eh?' said the canon.

'Oh no,' said Harry. 'For one thing,' he added, 'I like staying there, and, if I pinched his £10,000, that would come to an end, wouldn't it?'

'There are some people who never allow themselves bad motives for what they do. You seem to be a person who won't allow yourself a good motive for anything you do.'

'Anyway,' said Harry, 'I've got £20,000 which I can't spend at the moment; what's the good of another £10,000?'

'Well,' said the canon, 'you seem to have managed to spend £40,000 without much difficulty.'

'I had some difficulty,' said Harry, 'it wasn't all that easy, but I did manage it in the end. And without giving too much away.'

'So you gave some away?' said the canon.

'If you want to know,' said Harry, 'I gave some to the N.S.P.C.C., an institution which has no business to exist in this day and age. Don't you think it's fantastic that there is a private society to prevent cruelty to children? In the Welfare State too. I'd have thought that one of the first duties of the state was to see that children were protected.'

'I quite agree,' said the canon, 'but there isn't enough money to pay the police force properly, as it is. You've heard nothing more about your bank robber friend?'

'Not a thing,' said Harry. 'I wish I had.'

'Did you feel frightened all the time you were out?'

'Not all the time, but a good deal of it. It's a terrible thing, fear. I can't stand it.'

'You stood it in the war.'

'I had to, but I haven't got to now, and I won't. I daren't walk down a street without looking all round me to see if he's there. I daren't open the door without wondering if he's arrived at last. When I answer the telephone I wonder if it will be his voice that I hear. Believe me, I wouldn't give up the fleshpots or my young woman without a very good reason. But the absence of fear makes up for the lot. Have you never been frightened?'

'Of course I have,' said the canon, 'often, but only momentarily from time to time. A near-miss in a car, or during the war by a bomb. I've nothing hanging over my head, like you have. I quite agree, I'd hate that. You're frightened of dying, Harry, I suppose?'

'Not in the ordinary way, not by natural causes. I don't want a hole made in my heart before my time, and I most certainly don't want to be bashed up first.'

'But death by shooting,' said the canon, 'is preferable to death by a lingering disease.'

'I haven't got a lingering disease as far as I know,' said Harry. 'If I had, I might agree with you. I'm a pretty healthy chap with a good many years left. I won't say I'm in my prime but I don't want to be cut off unnaturally. I hate the idea. It's frustrating. So here we are again.'

'But, once they've caught the fellow, you won't want to come back, will you?'

'I suppose not.'

'But you're bound to come back unless you lead a different kind of life. What about this fear that you're so frightened of? When you are in the middle of one of your long firm larks, don't you start to get worried that you'll meet a policeman at the next corner who'll ask you if you aren't Harry Woodstock and tell you that he's got a warrant for your arrest?'

'You've got a point there,' said Harry. 'I'll just have to be more careful.'

'But they're bound to catch up with you in the end,' said the canon, 'it's only a question of time. A man with your record can't get away with it for long.'

'Well, I've got away with it in the past, sometimes,' said Harry.

'What's the longest time?'

'Two years.'

'Two years out and three years in,' said the canon, 'doesn't seem to be a very good bargain from your point of view.'

'I tell you,' said Harry, 'I'll be a bit more careful in future. I'll have a few more escape routes planned. Like this last time. I needn't have been convicted.'

'But you didn't get away with anything,' said the canon. 'You wouldn't make much of a living on that sort of fraud. Face the truth, Harry. As you say, you've got a good many more years yet to live. Why not live them in peace? Just imagine what the future will be, as you get older and older and less competent to commit your various crimes. In and out of gaol the whole time, and the older you get, the more you'll be in gaol. I quite understand your preferring to be in gaol now than to be free, because at the moment you're not free out of gaol, not free from fear anyway. That's a perfectly logical point of view. And, of course, if they never catch the man, you may have to spend your life in prison. But suppose they do catch him, surely you've had enough by now. Surely the time has come for you to make a break. You can have a whole new life in front of you, with no more fear. Just think of that, Harry. No more fear. You'll be like a cripple who's suddenly been cured. You'll be able to use your brains and your limbs as much as you like. No more preparing of escape routes. No more trials at the Old Bailey. No more verdicts. No more journeys to prison. No more releases from prison. Instead you can have all the fun. Theatres. Yes, women too. Music, sport. Any of the things you enjoy outside prison. All waiting for you round the corner.'

'And work too,' said Harry, 'waiting for me round the corner.'

'You have to do a bit of work here: not enough, I agree. And pretty soul-destroying on the whole. But outside there are all sorts of things you can do. With your capital you could—' but the canon paused.

'There's the rub,' said Harry. 'It isn't my capital. Are you advising me to use it?'

'I can't stop you using it,' said the canon, 'and although your only true peace will be if you hand it back, if you are going to spend it on yourself it's far better that you should spend it on a legitimate business than on another of your fraudulent schemes.'

'I think I might start up as an estate agent,' said Harry, 'then I can go either way.'

'What d'you mean by that?' said the canon.

'I can be respectable or not, can't I? Estate agents don't have to be registered, but they ought to be. Tell you what, here's an idea. Suppose I started a fraudulent estate agency in a really big way. Duped scores of small, unsuspecting people to give me their business and then walked away with it. That might give the public just the shock they need to force Parliament to do something about it. If I did that quite deliberately for that purpose, that would be what you might call a moral crime, wouldn't it?'

'Yes, if you handed back your ill-gotten gains at the end, it would be. But it's a dangerous way of getting reform, as one or two people have found in the past. I believe there was once a Mr Stead who got three months for proving how easy it was to procure a girl in furtherance of his campaign to prevent that sort of crime. You'd probably get three years again.'

'But I should have the satisfaction of being a pioneer,' said Harry. 'In fact they might call the Act "Harry Woodstock's Act". That would be rather nice. I'd leave my imprint on society in that way.'

'You're not being serious, I suppose?' said the canon.

'Of course not,' said Harry. 'The only imprints I'm going to leave on society are my fingerprints. I've no ambition to be a hero, or to have a statue somewhere. The only time I ever do anything good is when I can't help it.'

'That's nonsense, and you know it,' said the canon. 'By the way, would you let me meet your colonel some time?'

'Not if you told him who I was,' said Harry.

'Of course I wouldn't,' said the canon.

'D'you mean you wouldn't tell him the truth?' asked Harry. 'Who's slipping now?'

'You're quite right,' said the canon. 'If he asked me who you were, I should have to tell him.'

'Well, he won't ask you that,' said Harry, 'because he thinks he knows who I am.'

'I don't have to *volunteer* that you're an impostor.'

'He knows me now as Mr Princewig,' said Harry. 'The bank who chucked my money back at me know me as Mr Stout, and the safe deposit people know me as Mr Heape.

Now I come to think of it, Woodstock will be quite all right with the colonel, because he knew me as that, and I merely told him that I've changed my name because a relative left me some money. I'll arrange a tea party when I come out.'

'Would you mind if I went to see him while you're still in here?' asked the canon.

'Why do you want to?' said Harry. 'All part of your plan for the reformation of Harry Woodstock?'

'Certainly,' said the canon.

'I don't see why it should do any harm,' said Harry. 'Go along if you like. Introduce yourself. I'm on a secret mission at the moment, so that should be easy for you.'

The canon decided to pay a call on the other Albany. Unannounced he went up to the colonel's flat and rang the bell. The colonel opened the door.

'The cloth, eh?' he said. 'Subscription or something?'

'No, sir,' said the canon. 'I've come about a mutual friend of ours.'

'Why not say common,' said the colonel, 'if that's what you mean?'

'Very well, sir,' said the canon, 'a common friend of ours, Harry Woodstock.'

'Come in,' said the colonel. 'He saved my life.'

This was the first time that the canon had learned about Harry's exploit during the war, and his opinion of him, always high, rose still higher. He invited the colonel to tell him the circumstances.

'Certainly, sir,' said the colonel, 'but first of all, may I know whom I have the pleasure of addressing?'

'I'm Canon Abdale,' said the canon.

'Well, I'm Colonel Brookside,' said the colonel. 'So now we know where we are. Come in please, canon, and sit you down. Now I want you to follow this carefully.'

The canon was looking round the room.

'I said carefully, canon. If I'm going to expend my oxygen or nitrogen or whatever it is in telling you all about it, I do hope you'll have the goodness to listen, and listen carefully.'

'I am very sorry,' said the canon. 'Of course I will.'

'I hope you mean it,' said the colonel. 'Now look. This cigarette box is battalion headquarters. Do you know what battalion headquarters are, anyway?'

'I have an idea,' said the canon. 'I was a chaplain myself to a battalion.'

'Good,' said the colonel. 'Then we'll know what we're talking about. Now, this is battalion headquarters here. No, here. No, this table isn't much good, I'll get another one.'

He got another table more to his liking and put down the cigarette box on it.

'Now, I was going forward to make a recce. You know what a recce is? Harry's job was to stay behind and brew up when I came back. I took a subaltern and a lance-corporal with me. Some people would say that it's not the job of a C.O. to make a recce. Well, they're quite right. But this was very important, and I hadn't got an officer in the battalion I was prepared to trust it to. And in my view I was expendable. There were plenty of regular officers like me at the time. A hundred yards ahead of us there was a minefield. With, I should say, five hundred bloody great anti-personnel mines. I apologise for the language, canon, but, if you were in a battalion, you've heard worse than that.'

'I still hear worse than that,' said the canon.

'Good,' said the colonel. 'Bad language never did anyone any harm. Now, the sappers had gone out and made a path through this minefield. Big enough for two men to get through. Either walking or lying down. We went through that path safely enough, found out what we wanted and started to come back. And then somehow or other we were heard. They proceeded to put down everything on us. Shells, machine guns, mortars and God knows what. We were all wounded, and I couldn't move. The other two could just move but they couldn't carry me, so I told them to get back as best they could. And they beat it. Well, beat it isn't properly the word for somebody crawling on his belly at the rate of about a yard a minute. Eventually they got back and told Harry. By this time it was starting to get light, and the enemy's O.P.s (observation posts to you) could actually see the path through the minefield. As soon as Harry started to come down it, they put down everything they'd got. And that ought to have been the end of Harry. But it wasn't. I forget what the statistics are, but the number of shells and bullets it takes to kill one man is quite phenomenal. How they missed him I don't know. Nor does he. Just before dawn I found him next to me, safe and sound. He wasn't even scratched. He caught hold of me and dragged me all the way to safety. Why we weren't both killed I don't know. I stopped another bit, but Harry was still all right, and we got back to B.H.Q. with him only out of breath. I was in quite a bad way, but they got me out of the line, and I fully recovered eventually. People have got V.C.s for less. What d'you think Harry got?'

'I've no idea,' said the canon.

'Nothing,' said the colonel. 'Bloody nothing. And it wasn't for want of trying, I can assure you. First of all I wasn't in a condition to report for some time. That wouldn't have mattered. But my face didn't fit in brigade. The brigade-major came to see me while I was in hospital. The oily sod. I'm very sorry, canon, that is going a bit too far. No, damn it, it isn't; he *was* an oily sod. "How nice to see you, colonel," he said. "You mean you like to see me in bed?" I answered. "Not at all, colonel. I do hope your wounds are progressing favourably." "Thank you," I said. "Not at all. The brigadier particularly asked me to give you his good wishes. But would you mind if I spoke business?" "I can't imagine why else you came," I said. "It's about your report about Private Woodstock. You were pretty badly wounded, you know, colonel." "Thank you for telling me," I said. "Is your recollection of everything quite clear?" "Not everything," I said, "what d'you expect? There was a bloody great battle going on." "Quite so," said the brigade-major. "Everything was a bit hazy and unreal, I imagine?" "Not everything," I said, "some things." "How much do you weigh, colonel? Or rather how much did you weigh at the time?" "What the hell has that got to do with it?" I asked. "The brigadier wanted to know, and it's not on your papers." "My religion is C. of E." I said, "and my height five foot, eleven and a half." "And your weight, colonel?" persisted the brigade-major. "I don't know. Twelve stone or something like it, I suppose." "That's stripped, I imagine? In your clothes and boots and so on it would be a good deal more?" "All right, it would be a good deal more," I said. "So what?" "And you weren't able to walk?" persisted the brigade-major. "Of course I wasn't able to walk. Nobody could have walked. It would have been suicide to have walked." "But even if it wouldn't have been, you couldn't have walked owing to your wounds." "That's true," I said. "The brigadier finds it difficult to believe how a man of Harry Woodstock's physique could have dragged you along the ground five hundred yards." "Well, he did," I said. "That's in my report, isn't it?" "Oh yes, it's in your report, colonel, but the brigadier feels this must have been one of the things you're a little bit hazy about." "If he hadn't pulled me along," I told the brigade-major, "I should still have been there. But under the ground, not on it." "You've no witnesses, I suppose?" said the brigade-major. "I have got witnesses. I've got myself, and I've got Harry Woodstock." "Well, I can't very well ask him," said the brigade-major. "It would be too embarrassing." "I'm a witness, aren't I?" I said. "Oh, of course," said the brigade-major, "of course you are, colonel. But a very badly wounded witness. Possibly you weren't quite as far as you thought from battalion headquarters when you got hit." "Possibly I was in the Andes," I said, "but I wasn't. I was at least five hundred yards away from battalion headquarters, and Harry Woodstock pulled me all the way there." "Well I'll tell the brigadier," said the brigade-major. "I'm sure you'll understand, colonel, that there are so many awards to be given after a battle like this, that it is possible that in all the circumstances the brigadier may not feel justified in acceding to your recommendation." "You tell the brigadier," I said – this time I actually saw him take out a pencil and notebook and then he said: "Yes, colonel, I'm ready to take down what I am to tell the brigadier." Well, I didn't want a court martial, and once again I had to pipe down. "Tell the brigadier, please," I said, "I shall be most disappointed if an award is not made to Private Woodstock." "Of course," said the brigade-major, "and so will he. And so will I. But in a war there are so many valiant deeds which go unrewarded. I do hope you'll soon be better." That was the last time I saw the brigade-major. I knew what was going to happen. At least I didn't. I thought they must put him in for a mention.'

'It was a very brave deed,' said the canon.

'It was a bloody marvel,' said the colonel. 'Please forgive me, canon, but you know I've an almost irresistible urge to swear when one of your kidney comes in front of me.'

'It takes a lot of people like that,' said the canon.

'I'm a churchman myself,' said the colonel, 'but, to be quite frank, on the whole I don't like parsons. Nothing personal, you know. Some of them remind me of the brigade-major.

They're not all like that, of course, some of them are good fellows.'

'How nice of you to think so,' said the canon.

'I'm sorry Harry isn't here,' said the colonel. 'He's had to go off on business.'

'Quite,' said the canon.

'He's done bloody marvellously since the war. But perhaps you don't know what he's worth now?'

'I believe he's got control of quite a lot of money,' said the canon.

'He could buy me up ten times over,' said the colonel. 'I couldn't make out why a chap of such capability should only be a private soldier. I only discovered the reason a short while ago. But, dear me, I can't tell you.'

Suddenly a suspicion crossed the colonel's mind. He'd never seen this canon before. He didn't know much about espionage and counter-espionage. But he did know that people went in for it in all sorts of guises. Why had this parson suddenly come to him? In all probability he was snooping. He thought for a moment or two.

'You're a canon, are you?' he said.

'Yes.'

'Anything to prove it?'

'I'm not sure that I have at the moment,' said the canon. 'My driving licence. Oh no, I'm afraid I've left that at home.'

'Most unfortunate,' said the colonel. 'You'd like to know where Harry Woodstock is at the moment, wouldn't you?'

'I know where he is,' said the canon.

'You know?'

'Certainly.'

'Then what have you come here for?'

'To see you, colonel.'

'Why didn't you write or ring up first?'

'I thought you wouldn't mind if I just called. And you didn't seem to mind until a few seconds ago. Have I done anything to offend you?'

'If you're a foreign agent,' said the colonel, 'you'll get no change out of me.'

'A foreign agent,' said the canon. 'What on earth are you talking about, colonel?'

'I know what I'm talking about,' said the colonel, 'and I think you know too. I don't believe you're a canon at all.'

On this occasion the colonel had taken the plunge which he would have liked to have taken when speaking to the brigade major. On that occasion reasons of military discipline prevented him. On this occasion there was no such obstacle. And he took a chance, and made his allegation.

'I can only say that I am,' said the canon.

'Prove it,' said the colonel. 'Prove you're a canon.'

'Well,' said the canon, 'you can ring up the Bishop of London's office if you like. They'll tell you that I am Canon Abdale.'

'I'm not saying there isn't a Canon Abdale,' said the colonel. 'But are you he? I *will* ring the Bishop of London's office.'

He looked in the telephone book, found the number and dialled it.

'This is Colonel Brookside speaking from Albany, Piccadilly. I have someone who calls himself Canon Abdale with me. Have you anybody in your office who would recognise his voice, please? I don't mind if it is unusual. There are a lot of things in life that are unusual. But, if you want to know, I think this man may be a spy. Now kindly tell me, have you anybody in the office who would recognise Canon Abdale's voice? Not at the moment? In a couple of hours? Fat lot of use that'll be. I'm not going to keep him here a couple of hours. Thank you.'

The colonel hung up the receiver.

'Anyone else to try? The Archbishop of Canterbury, d'you think?'

'I shouldn't like to trouble His Grace,' said the canon.

'What about the Lord Mayor of London?' said the colonel.

'Colonel,' said the canon, 'I think I ought to warn you that, if you start telling people on the telephone that I'm a spy, you may land yourself in legal proceedings. Let me make it plain that I should be very sorry indeed to institute such proceedings. But there must be a limit to all this, you know.'

'We ought to have identity cards,' grumbled the colonel.

'If I were a spy,' said the canon, 'my identity card would be forged. That, I believe, is simple enough.'

'But, if you weren't a spy, you'd have an identity card which would show who you were,' said the colonel.

'Yes,' said the canon, 'but how could you tell the difference?'

The colonel thought for a moment.

'I see,' he said. 'D'you give me your word of honour as a man of God that you are Canon Abdale?'

'Most certainly I do,' said the canon. 'But, colonel, if I were not Canon Abdale, and if I were in fact a foreign agent, I should equally be prepared to make such a declaration.'

'I see,' said the colonel, and again lapsed into silence. 'Well, how do we solve this one?' he asked eventually.

'If you care to come back with me to my hotel,' said the canon, 'you can satisfy yourself, I think, by speaking to my wife and looking at various letters and documents that I have there that I am in fact Canon Abdale. But, of course, I might have forged documents and a forged wife.'

'Are you laughing at me, sir?' asked the colonel.

The canon thought for a moment. 'Yes,' he said, 'I'm afraid I am. I apologise.'

'How can I tell whether to accept your apology,' said the colonel, 'until I know who you are?'

'Come back to my hotel for tea,' said the canon. 'And bring a policeman with you if you like. Now I'm laughing again. I apologise again.'

'It's these films and books, I see and read too many of them,' said the colonel. 'They're bad for people, they shouldn't be allowed.'

'But I see and read them too,' said the canon. 'They don't seem to do me any harm.'

'If you're in the secret service,' said the colonel, 'they wouldn't.'

'I'm not.'

'I've still only your word for that. What about your bank manager? He'd recognise your voice, wouldn't he?'

'He might,' said the canon, 'but I'm not at all sure that he would. I've only met him twice.'

'One of the cashiers or the accountant, or someone in the bank?'

'I don't go very often,' said the canon. 'I haven't many financial transactions. My account, I'm afraid, is lamentably small. Unlike that of Canon Abdale of the Secret Service. Another laugh I'm afraid, and another apology.'

'Look, sir,' said the colonel, 'either you're a foreign agent or you're not. If you're a foreign agent, at any rate I can respect you. You're only doing your job, and it can be a dangerous job too. But, if you are who you say you are, you've been extremely offensive to me.'

'I have been a little offensive to you, colonel,' said the canon, 'but not perhaps without some provocation. If I had challenged you with not being a colonel and being a foreign agent, you wouldn't be very pleased, would you?'

'I could prove my identity, sir, which is more than you can.'

'Well, prove it, please, colonel,' said the canon. 'Have you got your army discharge papers on you?'

'Certainly not. I keep them at the bank. But I've got heaps of letters addressed to me.'

'So would an agent, colonel. He's got to have a sufficient cover.'

'Well, you haven't.'

'That suggests I'm not an agent, doesn't it?'

'I've got a cheque book.'

'What does that prove, colonel? What about your driving licence?'

'I don't drive,' said the colonel.

'I tell you what,' said the canon, 'what about a battalion photograph?'

'I haven't got one here,' said the colonel.

'Well, you're at home and I'm not,' said the canon. 'You seem to be worse off than I am.'

'The porter downstairs could identify me.'

'Of course he could, colonel. And there's no doubt whatever that, if you're a foreign agent, you're masquerading as Colonel Brookside. Just as, if I'm a foreign agent, I'm masquerading as Canon Abdale.'

'I've been here ten years,' said the colonel.

'How long was Mr Philby employed by the Government?' asked Canon Abdale. 'Some agents are fixtures for quite a long time.'

'You accuse me in front of a third party of being a foreign spy,' said the colonel, 'and I shall sue you. I'll sue you very hard indeed. I'll claim the highest damages known to the law. I'm a British subject by birth. I joined the army when I was eighteen. I am an ex-regular officer. I was given an O.B.E. No, you can forget that, I've tried to.'

'But you're not married, colonel.'

'What of that?'

'Foreign agents often aren't married.'

'How d'you know?'

'It's what I've read,' said the canon.

'You can ring up my wine merchant. He'll recognise my voice. He'll tell you who I am.'

'But, colonel,' said the canon, 'if you are a foreign agent masquerading as a colonel, how will that help me? Naturally you've settled yourself in. You've got all your tradesmen and acquaintances and other people to think that you are a genuine colonel. And, if in fact you're a foreign agent, they've just been deceived, as I may be.'

'I give you my word as an officer and a gentleman,' said the colonel, 'that I am an officer and a gentleman.'

'Just as I gave you my word,' said the canon. 'But, if in fact we're foreign agents, that's exactly what we would do. Swear on the Bible or anything else that was required of us. Perhaps we don't know it but we both are foreign agents. After all we're both getting on a bit. Memories aren't quite so good as they were, and play tricks with us. I may have lived the life of a canon so long that I really think I am one. You may have lived the life of a colonel for so long that you really think you are one. But in point of fact we're nothing of the kind. We receive our salaries from a man in dark glasses outside a doubtful restaurant in Soho.'

'It's a dangerous job being an agent,' said the colonel.

'Have you found it so?' said the canon.

'I didn't say I was one. I merely said it was dangerous.'

'Well, we can agree upon that,' said the canon.

After a few moments of silence the colonel said:

'I don't like not being believed. If you will agree that I am Colonel Brookside, I'll agree that you're Canon Abdale.'

But before the canon could answer there was a ring at the bell.

6 *Lady Mary*

The colonel answered it. It was an elegantly dressed woman of about his own age.

'Tea and toast,' she said.

'Why didn't you tell me you were coming?'

'I'll answer over the tea and toast,' she said. 'Oh, you've got someone,' she added. 'Shall I go away after the tea and toast?'

'This is—,' began the colonel, and paused. He looked at the canon, who nodded and mouthed: 'Done.'

'This is Canon Abdale,' continued the colonel. 'My cousin, Lady Mary Broadway.'

'A canon?' queried Lady Mary. 'Major or minor, might I ask? And exactly what is a major canon? And what does a canon do anyway? Are you attached to a cathedral, or have you got a living, or what? . . .'

The canon was prepared to answer each of Lady Mary's questions as it was asked. But, when he realised that she was going from one question to another without giving him the opportunity, he remained silent. At the end of another dozen questions she said: 'How do you do?' *That* at any rate the canon could answer.

'How do you do?' he said.

'Were you at school together or something?' said Lady Mary. 'Oh no, you're much too young.'

'We have a mutual friend in my batman,' said the colonel.

life, that was just during the war. He's a very distinguished businessman. Goes all over the world. He's worth millions.'

'I'd like to meet him,' said Lady Mary.

'He saved my life,' said the colonel.

'I'd still like to meet him,' she said.

'He's probably in China at the moment,' said the colonel. 'Remarkable man. I can still hardly credit it that during the war he was just a private soldier, and my batman.'

'Have you a bit of dry bread?' said Lady Mary. 'These biscuits are quite uneatable.'

'It's a bit stale, I'm afraid,' said the colonel.

'You keep that for your guests too, do you?' said Lady Mary.

'To tell you the truth,' said the colonel, 'I don't eat much here myself. I used to when I had a housekeeper, but, when she left, I found it easier to go out. What are you doing in London?'

'Calling on you, of course. I came up to do some shopping, but there's simply nothing to buy. Nothing at a reasonable price, that is. What is this Prices and Income Board? Whenever I go into a shop I find the price has gone up, and nobody seems to do anything about it. I suppose nobody bothers. It would be fun to call a policeman sometimes.'

'I can call spirits from the vasty deep,' said the canon.

'You're quite right,' said Lady Mary. 'That's another disgrace. High prices and no policemen. In my young days it was a very comforting thought to know that, if you shouted for help, there'd be a policeman with you in no time. I almost forget what one looks like, except on television. There are plenty of them there, I grant you. Have you ever been to prison, canon?'

'Oh yes,' said the canon, 'I go quite often.'

'I'd like to go, I think,' said Lady Mary. 'I think everyone should, don't you? I mean how are we to know whether prison is the right treatment for people if we don't go there ourselves?'

'I meant as a visitor,' said the canon.

'So did I,' said Lady Mary. 'I didn't really imagine that you could have a canon with a record. But I suppose you have some criminals in your ranks.'

'There are criminals in spirit in every walk of life,' said the canon.

'Oh, spirit,' said Lady Mary. 'I haven't time to go into metaphysics and all that. The practical problems of the day are enough for me. Do many parsons go to prison? I mean, are they sent to prison?'

'Not many,' said the canon.

'How many canons?'

'None that I know of.'

'How does one get to prison?' said Lady Mary. 'I mean, to visit it. What should I do?'

'Write to the Home Office, I should think,' said the canon. 'But it's not all that easy. It's not like the zoo.'

'George,' said Lady Mary, 'your visitor's being rude to me. Protect me from him.'

'What did he say?' asked the colonel.

'He suggested that I had a morbid desire to go and look at human beings whom we've locked up.'

'I didn't hear you,' said the colonel, 'but how dare you, sir! You come here uninvited and insult my guests. What you said is completely untrue.'

'Oh no,' said Lady Mary, 'it's completely true. That's why I'm so angry. I shall have to take my hat off. Where's the bedroom?'

The colonel showed her to it and then came back to the canon.

'I think I told you,' he said when he came back, 'that I'm a pretty offensive person.'

'You've been very courteous to me,' said the canon.

'I'll soon put that right,' said the colonel. 'What the devil d'you mean by insulting my cousin!'

'I'm extremely sorry.'

'Words!' said the colonel. 'Parsons are never short of words.'

'Nor, if I may say so,' said the canon, slightly nettled, 'is your cousin.'

'How dare you, sir!' said the colonel. 'You come here unasked, tell me that I'm a spy, and say that Lady Mary Broadway talks too much. Whose business is it, may I ask, if she does talk too much? And whose flat is this?'

'I apologise,' said the canon.

'That's the second time,' said the colonel. 'You apologise a damned sight too often. That's your stock in trade, I suppose. Hurt someone's feelings, get your satisfaction, and then say you're sorry. I bet you only do it to stop them knocking you on the jaw. I've a very good mind to, except that that sort of thing isn't done in Albany.'

'Would you care to come outside, sir?' said the canon.

'You want to provoke me, do you?' said the colonel.

'Yes,' said the canon, 'I do rather. Am I succeeding?'

'You're behaving disgracefully,' said the colonel. 'I shall report you to your bishop.'

'To whom should I report you?' asked the canon. 'Your major-general? I'm afraid I'm not up in the army establishment. Perhaps I'd better go.'

'Yes, sir,' said the colonel, 'you had. But not till I've told you what I think of you.'

'Keep that,' said the canon, 'for your officers in the next war,' and he left.

7 *The Prison Outside*

Some little time later Colonel Brookside and Lady Mary were in a lakeland hotel in Cumberland supposedly on holiday. The colonel sat miserably in a chair in the lounge watching the rain pour down. Opposite him was his cousin.

'Why did we come here?' he said plaintively.

'For a change,' said Lady Mary. 'It's better to watch the rain pouring on the mountains and the valleys than on Piccadilly.'

'I don't see why,' said the colonel. 'There are pretty girls in Piccadilly.'

'Not when it rains,' said Lady Mary. 'They go inside. Now the mountains and the valleys stay outside. Look at them. They're glorious.'

'It's no virtue in them,' said the colonel. 'They can't help it.'

'I didn't say it was a virtue in them,' said Lady Mary. 'I said it was an advantage to us. Now pull yourself together and look. Look at those colours. Look at the light on that mountain.'

'There's precious little light,' said the colonel.

'Look at that dark cloud over the mountain. Thundering, menacing. Isn't it wonderful?'

'I've been looking at it all too long,' said the colonel. 'It's horrible.'

'If there were blue sky and sun, you'd say it was too hot.'

'If I said it was too hot, it *would* be too hot,' said the colonel.

'But there's no reason for it to be too hot. You can have a fine day without it being too hot. But you can't have a wet day without it being too wet, and this is too wet, too bloody wet, if I may say so.'

'No, you may not,' said Lady Mary. 'You know I dislike you swearing.'

'Well, I don't know why we came here at all,' said the colonel. 'I saw all the mountains and valleys and skies and clouds I wanted to when I was in the army. All the dawns and sunsets too. What's there left for a chap like me once he comes out of the Service? I'm good for nothing. Thirty years of my life given in the service of the country, and what have I got at the end of it? A miserable pittance of a pension. If I'd been good-tempered in the army, I certainly would be bad-tempered now. Look at the difference between me and that fellow Harry Woodstock. He was my batman, and now he owns half the businesses in the world. He's got plenty to do, plenty to think about. His life's not wasted. He doesn't have to look at thundering, menacing clouds and make do with them. He charters a plane and goes off to Japan or the Balearic Islands, or whatever you like. What a man! I hope he'll be back in London soon. I miss him, Mary. You get used to a batman, you know, and I've missed him ever since the end of the war. And what I like about the fellow is that success hasn't spoiled him at all. He treats me just as he did when I was a battalion commander and he was just a private soldier. No false airs and graces about him.'

'Yes,' said Lady Mary, 'he sounds a nice little man. Not the tycoon type at all.'

'He isn't,' said the colonel. ' "Tycoon" has an unpleasant flavour about it. People who grind the masses into the ground so long as they get a huge profit. People who ride roughshod over the rights of others. People whose only concern is their own personal wealth, and their own personal importance. Woodstock's not like that at all. Pity there aren't more like him. He's a sense of fun too. We'd many a good joke together when things were pretty lively. I remember once when we were both half-knocked out by a shell. We weren't wounded, but just blown about the place. When we were feeling a bit more like ourselves, I said to him: "Now, Private Woodstock, make me laugh." What do you think he said?'

'I can't imagine,' said Lady Mary.

The colonel paused for a moment or two.

'Good God,' he said eventually, 'neither can I. What the hell was it? I know I laughed till I cried. I know, I've got it. He said: "What's the difference between a near miss and a bull's eye?"'

'And what is it?' asked Lady Mary. 'I'm waiting to laugh till I cry.'

The colonel looked thoughtful. 'Damn it, I've forgotten that now. A near miss and a bull's eye. What *is* the difference? I wish he were here, he could tell us. I wonder where he is at the present moment. I wish I were there too, instead of in this confounded place.'

'You must be more philosophical, dear,' said his cousin. 'Like me.'

'Philosophy be damned,' said the colonel. 'I never did understand the stuff.' He called a waiter. 'I want to see the manager, please.'

It was a quarter of an hour before the manager arrived.

'You wanted to see me, sir?'

'I wanted to see you a quarter of an hour ago,' said the colonel.

'I'm afraid I wasn't in; I've only just got back.'

'Then the waiter should have told me so.'

'I'm sorry he didn't, sir.'

'The coffee was undrinkable this morning.'

'I thought you ordered tea, sir. That would account for it. I would find coffee undrinkable if I was expecting tea, or tea undrinkable if I was expecting coffee.'

'Or,' said the colonel, 'lime juice undrinkable if I was expecting bread and milk. I ordered coffee.'

'Tea, sir.'

'Coffee.'

'Tea. Well, which will you have tomorrow, sir?'

'The same as I ordered for today, please.'

'Well, that was tea, sir.'

'It was coffee, though it didn't taste like it.'

'I've explained that, sir. It wouldn't taste like coffee, if it was tea.'

'Perhaps,' said Lady Mary, 'it would simplify things if you sent both tea and coffee.'

'And I might pour out the wrong one,' said the colonel.

'Couldn't they be labelled?' said Lady Mary. 'In capital letters – Tea, Coffee.'

'Well,' said the colonel, 'can you rise to that?'

'Certainly, sir,' said the manager. 'I'm afraid we shall charge extra.'

'I thought your terms were inclusive,' said the colonel.

'So they are,' said the manager. 'I don't expect to supply tea which you're not going to drink, or coffee which you're not going to drink, in addition to tea which you are going to drink, or coffee which you are going to drink.'

'I don't think I shall drink either,' said the colonel. 'I shall leave today.'

'I'm afraid, sir, that you'll have to pay to the end of the week in that case. Unless, of course, we can let the rooms. It's such short notice, I doubt if we will be able to. Particularly in this weather.'

'Why refer to the weather?' said the colonel. 'That's really what's got me down. If the weather had been decent, the coffee wouldn't have seemed so bad.'

'The tea, you mean, sir. Do you really wish to leave today, sir?'

'I said so, didn't I?'

'Yes, sir. But you also said that you'd ordered coffee when you'd ordered tea.'

'You're a bit obstinate, aren't you?' said the colonel.

'Yes,' said the manager. 'I've often told myself I'm not really suited to this job. As far as I'm concerned the customer's more often wrong than we are and when he is, I shall say so. It really doesn't seem to make much difference. The takings are about the same as they were when the previous manager was here.'

'Does the proprietor know how you talk to your guests?' asked the colonel.

'She does,' said the manager, 'but she does the same herself. She's my wife, as a matter of fact. Well, are you going to leave, or aren't you? And do you want a car to take you to the station? There's only one train, and that's in an hour's time. Would you like to take sandwiches, or will you have something on the train?'

'I haven't said I'm going yet,' said the colonel. 'The truth of the matter is that I'm bored stiff.'

'Would a game of billiards be of any use to you, sir?'

'I don't play the game.'

'Table tennis, then, sir?'

'It used to be called ping-pong,' said the colonel.

'That was when it *was* ping-pong,' said the manager. 'It is now a highly skilled, quite exhausting game.'

'Do I look as though I want to play a highly skilled, quite exhausting game?' said the colonel.

'If you want me to be quite frank, sir,' said the manager, 'you don't look as though you wanted to play anything. You look as though you want to go and drown yourself.'

'That's how I feel,' said the colonel.

'There are plenty of facilities round here,' said the manager. 'The lake's only a quarter of a mile away. If I were you, sir,' he added, 'I should have a couple of dry Martinis before you go.'

'Tea and toast for me, please,' said Lady Mary.

'Why do you never have anything sensible?' said the colonel. 'Tea and toast, at this time of the day.'

'I could live on it,' said Lady Mary.

'You pretty well do,' said the colonel, 'as far as I can see.'

'And why not?' said the manager. 'Why shouldn't madam live on tea and toast if she wants to?'

'What the hell's that got to do with you?' said the colonel.

'Nothing much,' said the manager, 'but I was just joining in the conversation to be helpful. You said you were bored. I was trying to raise your spirits a little. I notice you did perk up a bit at the mention of a dry Martini.'

'What's the good of a mention?' said the colonel. 'Why don't you *do* something about it?'

'You haven't ordered it yet,' said the manager. 'If I brought it when you hadn't ordered it, you might say you didn't want it, and then I couldn't charge you for it. Inclusive terms don't include free dry Martinis.'

'I didn't ask for a free dry Martini,' said the colonel.

'You didn't ask for one at all,' said the manager.

'Will you have a drink with us?' said the colonel.

'That's very kind,' said the manager, 'yes, I will, please. May I have a large dry Martini?'

'A large one?'

'Yes, please. I find a small one merely whets the appetite, and it saves time if I have the two together.'

'I offered you one drink, not two,' said the colonel.

'As a matter of fact,' said the manager, 'there are many establishments where, if you order a dry Martini, you get a large one automatically.'

'Is this such an establishment?' asked the colonel.

'No, it isn't, as a matter of fact.'

'Then, what's that got to do with it?' asked the colonel.

'When you two boys have finished playing,' said Lady Mary, 'do you think I could have my tea and toast?'

'Immediately, madam,' said the manager, and went out.

'Not a bad fellow,' said the colonel, 'but how he manages to run an hotel, heaven alone knows. I think I shall send Harry Woodstock a wire to meet us somewhere. Damn it, I can't. I don't know where to send it to. He just turns up all of a sudden, and goes away all of a sudden. Well, I suppose that's how it is when millions depend upon what one man says or does, or where he is.'

'I should like to see that canon again,' said Lady Mary.

'He's not a canon,' said the colonel. 'He's a foreign agent. Now wait a moment,' he added, 'no, that was what I first thought. No, he is a canon.'

'How about inviting him to tea?' said Lady Mary.

'He was very rude about you, if my memory's correct,' said the colonel.

'Splendid,' said Lady Mary. 'I like him all the more. That's one of the things people like about you, dear. Look how the manager warmed to you the ruder you were to him.'

'He got a couple of drinks out of me,' said the colonel. 'If that's what you mean by "warming" to me. Damn it, do you think he'll bring one to me? I don't think I ordered one for myself. He's quite capable of just having a large one and giving me nothing.'

'So long as he brings my tea and toast. We did order that,' said Lady Mary.

But the manager did return with two dry Martinis and Lady Mary's tea and toast. As they had their first sip the manager said:

'This should put you in the mood, sir.'

'Mood for what?' said the colonel.

'I thought you were going to drown yourself.'

'It wouldn't do the hotel any good, would it? I'd leave a note behind saying why I did it.'

'I know the coroner here. He'd simply say "of unsound mind". Well, is your Martini all right, sir? I made it myself, as a matter of fact.'

'Yes,' said the colonel, 'I'm sorry to have to admit it is very good.'

'The tea and toast are excellent,' said Lady Mary, 'and it is tea, not coffee.'

'The same as I had this morning,' said the colonel. 'But it should have been coffee, not tea.'

'Well, we'll put that right in the morning,' said the manager. 'Coffee for you, sir, and tea for madam.'

'I think the rain's lessening slightly,' said the colonel.

'That's the dry Martini,' said the manager. 'In fact it's raining as hard as ever. But it doesn't seem to matter as much. That's the one thing drink will do; disperses worry. It's no good for anything serious but the petty things in life, they disappear as soon as I have a couple of Martinis inside me. I now feel I can put up with guests who say they've ordered tea when in fact they've ordered coffee, and vice versa.'

'If I may say so,' said the colonel, 'you don't "put up" with guests at all.'

'No, I suppose you're right,' said the manager. 'I don't even endure them.'

'Have you ever thought of advertising?' said Lady Mary. 'It would be a new idea – the hotel where the manager and not the guest is always right.'

'Not a bad idea,' said the manager. 'We might try it some time. Will you have another drink, sir?'

'That's very kind of you.'

'I hope it is,' said the manager. 'If you find it on your bill, just let me know.'

By the time the colonel had had three large dry Martinis he was feeling a little better.

'If you'll forgive me now, sir,' said the manager, 'I must go and console some of the other guests.'

'For the weather,' asked the colonel, 'or for the service and food in this hotel?'

'That depends on the guest, sir,' said the manager. 'There are those who don't notice what you throw at them, or how you throw it. And there are those who are more particular and who say they've asked for tea when you give them coffee. If I may say so, sir, you'd run a hotel extraordinarily well. The more you charge and the more offensive you are to your guests, the more they want to come. I tried an experiment once of saying we were full up for a month when we weren't. You've no idea how much people want what they can't get. For the next three months, we were absolutely packed out. The theatres might try it.'

'Then they'd play to empty seats,' said Lady Mary.

'Oh no, madam,' said the manager. 'What you'd do would be to give the cast a holiday. Say you were booked out and put out the House Full notices every night for a week. Meantime the public are clamouring to get in and the cast are having a beautiful holiday. Put up a House Full notice in the most expensive restaurant in London and they'll flock to it, even if the cooking's no better than it is here. If you want to publicise a new artist, put up red tabs on all his pictures. There'd be an immediate demand for them.'

'Would that be honest?' asked Lady Mary.

'Of course not,' said the manager. 'But who's honest in business? I'm certainly not.'

'Well, you're wrong,' said the colonel. 'I know a man who's made his way from nothing to the top of the tree, and he's as honest as the day is long.'

'How well do you know him, sir?'

'Well enough,' said the colonel. 'We served together during the war.'

'Oh, war is different,' said the manager. 'In a war you have to get down to brass tacks. You might even have to be honest. When it's a matter of life or death, you might even have to tell the truth.'

'This man was my batman, and he saved my life. Before the war, he was nothing at all. Now he could buy up this hotel ten times over.'

'Do you think he'd make me an offer?' said the manager.

'If you really want to sell,' said the colonel, 'I'll ask him. Fifty thousand pounds or so is nothing to him.'

'Well, I'll bear it in mind in case I get bored.'

'Do. Drop me a line. I hope I'll be seeing him soon. He usually turns up once every few years, and I haven't seen him for a couple of years now.'

'What sort of business is he in, might I ask?'

'I don't exactly know,' said the colonel, 'but every kind, I should think. Oil, textiles, machinery, minerals – pretty well everything, I should say. I expect he's got a merchant bank as well.'

'And you say he was a batman during the war?'

'Certainly.'

'How did he get started, then? Putting his hand in someone's till?'

'What a monstrous thing to say,' said the colonel. 'He could sue you for slander, if I told him. I don't suppose he'd bother. The money wouldn't be any use to him. I wanted to invest ten thousand pounds with him, but he wouldn't take it. He said the only thing they weren't short of was money. He's the sort of chap we want to have in the government, running the country, when all the chaps we have are failures. They're no good at anything else, so they go in for politics. They're all scrambling to get to the top, over each other's backs, and they don't particularly mind which back they stab in the process.'

'Have you never considered going into politics yourself, sir?'

'Certainly not,' said the colonel. 'It's a dirty game.'

'Well, if somebody didn't go in for it, we'd have nobody to look after us, would we?'

'You can say that about anything,' said the colonel. 'If somebody didn't look after the lavatories, we'd have no lavatory attendants. But we have got lavatory attendants. And we've got politicians. And we've got lawyers. And now perhaps I might add, without offence, we have hotel keepers.'

'If I didn't run this hotel, or if somebody didn't run it, you'd have nowhere to stay.'

'So much the better,' said the colonel. 'Then we shouldn't have come to this god-forsaken place.'

'It's very nice when it isn't raining,' said Lady Mary.

'Well, it always is raining,' said the colonel. 'We haven't been able to go out for three whole days.'

'I could lend you an old macintosh, or an old hat,' said the manager.

'No doubt you could,' said the colonel. 'It's very nice of you. But I don't want to get wet, thank you very much. I like to walk out when the sun is shining high in the heaven and when there's a nice gentle breeze to prevent it from being too hot. That's my idea of a holiday in the country. Not being cooped up in a moth-eaten old inn.'

'Shall I decant another bottle of the burgundy for dinner?' asked the manager.

'What's that? How do I know, till I know what we're eating? That's the trouble with you fellows. You haven't got any palates.'

'Well, you're going to eat trout and saddle of lamb, if you can manage it,' said the manager.

'Whether or not I can manage it will depend on how it's cooked.'

'Well, it won't be cooked any better than usual – that I can promise you.'

'Will it be worse?'

'That's quite possible. They might burn the trout.'

'Well, we'll have half a bottle of that white stuff you call Meursault. I expect it was half Spanish, anyway. And a bottle of the red stuff which you call Burgundy. I suppose you know you can have red and white claret, as well as red and white Burgundy?'

'No, I didn't know that,' said the manager. 'Claret surely is claret colour?'

'Red claret is claret colour, and white claret is not.'

'But how can you have white claret?'

'Well, you can, that's all,' said the colonel. 'The Bordeaux wines are called Claret – some are white and some are red.'

'Do you charge for your lessons, sir?' asked the manager.

'You can put in a bottle free, if you like,' said the colonel.

'I'll make it half a bottle. You can have the Meursault with the compliments of the house.'

'That's because it's mostly Spanish, I suppose?'

'To tell you the truth, I haven't had it analysed. But I rely on the shippers, and I haven't had a complaint yet.'

'Of course you haven't had a complaint,' said the colonel. 'Nobody knows what he's drinking. If you give it a high-sounding enough name on the label and on the wine list, and charge enough for it, they'll think it's marvellous. In fact, it's Portuguese and Spanish mixed with a dash of French thrown in. That's one of the few things I do know something about: which is more than you can say for most wine waiters.'

'Well, you're quite right in the present case,' said the manager. 'If you want to know, our wine waiter who comes up to you so confidentially and describes all the beauties of different bottles of wine was the under-gardener. He doesn't know a bottle of Romanée Conti from a bottle of lemonade. But he's learned all the tricks of the trade, and he talks as if he knew as much as you do. "If I were you, sir," he says very softly, "I should have the '57, not the '59." The truth is, of course, that we've run out of the '59. Or alternatively it's better than the '57, and we want it for a few of the guests who know what they're drinking. He was a jolly good gardener, but he's just as good a wine waiter, and it isn't because we've got some grapes in the hothouse.'

'Are they muscat?' asked the colonel.

'No,' said the manager, 'I'm afraid not.'

'Then they're not worth eating,' said the colonel.

'You needn't worry about that,' said the manager. 'We keep them for the family. That's one thing you *can* get out of hotel businesses. You keep the best things for yourselves.'

'You mentioned Romanée Conti,' said the colonel. 'Do you really have any here?'

'Oh good gracious, no. I've got a few labels, but I wouldn't dare put them on. People who ask for Romanée Conti know what they're drinking.'

'Look,' said Lady Mary, 'it's almost stopped raining. Let's take a turn. Borrow that old hat and macintosh if the manager will still kindly lend it to you.'

'You're very welcome,' said the manager. 'It was left here by a man who didn't pay his bill, as a matter of fact.'

'I don't like wearing other people's hats,' said the colonel. 'I'll take an umbrella, thank you.'

At that moment, an extraordinary thing happened. The sun came out and the rain stopped completely.

'Let's go out before it changes its mind,' said Lady Mary. And out they went.

After they had been walking for about ten minutes, the colonel complained that the sun was too hot.

'There's an avenue of trees,' said Lady Mary. 'Let's go down there.'

They did so, and the colonel complained that the water from the trees was dripping down his neck.

8 *Who is My Neighbour?*

While the colonel was moaning about the weather the canon was visiting Harry at Albany, I.O.W.

'I've got some news for you,' he said. 'I hope you'll be pleased. I'm standing in for your chaplain here for a month.'

'That *is* good news,' said Harry. 'I hope I'll see a lot of you.'

'As much as I've time for,' said the canon.

'You may find some more worthwhile material,' said Harry.

When the canon called on Harry a week later he found him in an apparently rather troubled mood.

'What's up?' he asked.

'I've a problem,' said Harry.

'Can I help?'

'Everything I say to you is in confidence, isn't it?'

'Of course.'

'I suppose it's one of the oldest problems in the world. Who is my neighbour?'

'Everyone,' said the canon without hesitation.

'But supposing their claims conflict,' said Harry.

'How d'you mean?'

'Well,' said Harry, 'all my colleagues here are my neighbours, I assume.'

'Of course.'

'And so are you.'

'I hope so.'

'And so is the governor.'

'Quite.'

'Well,' said Harry, 'haven't I said enough by introducing the governor into the conversation to show that the claims might conflict? Supposing I saw a fellow prisoner beating up the governor. A fellow prisoner's my neighbour. I ought to help him, oughtn't I?'

'Don't be silly,' said the canon, 'it's in the long-term interests of your neighbour, the prisoner, that he should be prevented from assaulting your neighbour, the governor. And it's in the short-term and long-term interests of the governor that the assault should be prevented as quickly as possible.'

'All right,' said Harry. 'Supposing one of my neighbours plans to escape. Have I got a duty to grass?'

'Certainly not,' said the canon.

'Have I got a duty not to grass?'

The canon thought for a moment.

'I suppose it depends somewhat on the nature of the escape. If it involved hurting or killing a prison officer, you certainly haven't got a duty *not* to tell anybody about it.'

'Well then,' said Harry, 'have I got a duty *to* tell somebody about it? To grass on my neighbour?'

'If violence is intended,' said the canon, 'I think you must have.'

'When a man tries to escape,' said Harry, 'there may always be violence.'

'Who are you trying to tell me about?' asked the canon.

'I'm not trying to tell you about anyone,' said Harry.

'Well, you're trying to warn me about something,' said the canon. 'I'll have to be on the alert.'

'Well,' said Harry, 'if I have warned you, I'm guilty of talebearing.'

'To a very limited extent, yes,' said the canon. 'But you're in a very difficult position. Prisoners always are.'

'If an escape is planned,' persisted Harry, 'has a prisoner who knows about it a legal or moral duty to tell someone about it?'

'I don't think there's a legal duty,' said the canon. 'I don't know all the prison regulations, but I don't think there's any legal regulation that prisoners must give information about such matters.'

'Has he, then, a moral duty?'

'It's a very difficult question.'

'No one approves of a grass,' said Harry. 'You don't, do you?'

'No,' said the canon, 'I can't pretend I do.'

'Why don't you approve?' asked Harry. 'It can only be because we have a duty to our neighbours – not to grass.'

'But,' said the canon, 'you also have your duty to your neighbours – a moral duty – to help them carry out their work, namely to keep the prisoners in prison. In other words you have a moral duty to assist the prison officers and the governor to discharge their duties.'

'So,' said Harry, 'I have a moral duty both to the prisoners and to the governor. Which comes first?'

'I don't know,' said the canon, 'but I know which would come first with me if I were in your position.'

'I'm glad we agree about that,' said Harry. 'Now here's a further question. You believe in the truth, don't you?'

'Passionately,' said the canon.

'Suppose I'm asked about this. This is purely theoretical,' said Harry. 'Suppose I'm asked about this, what am I to say? Tell the truth?'

'Yes,' said the canon, 'you must always tell the truth.'

'Even if it gives away my friends, my neighbours?'

'Yes,' said the canon, 'even if it gives them away. In the short term I quite agree it will be a very unhappy experience for you.'

'How right you are,' said Harry. 'I may not live to have another such experience.'

'Are you going to explain?' asked the canon.

'I think I shall have to,' said Harry, 'but first of all I repeat that what I tell you, if I tell you anything, is in confidence, isn't it?'

'It is,' said the canon, 'subject to this. That if I knew that violence were intended towards anybody, I should have to take steps about it.'

'Then I'd better not tell you,' said Harry, 'because violence is intended towards somebody.'

'I see,' said the canon.

'If I thought that anything I told you could get any one of my neighbours here into trouble, I couldn't possibly tell you, could I?' said Harry.

'That,' said the canon, 'would depend. If murder or something of that sort were intended, I think you could and should.'

'No, it's not as bad as that,' said Harry. 'But once violence starts, you never know where it's going to lead. That's why I'm so frightened of it. I mean, if you just tie a chap up to a chair and gag him, he may die of fright. Or you might even suffocate him if you didn't know how to gag him properly. What d'you think of your choir?' he said, apparently changing the subject.

'Not bad,' said the canon. 'Indeed, pretty good. As you know, I've only had it for a very short time, but I should say it's one of the best prison choirs that I've come across.'

'Any new members since you first arrived?' asked Harry.

'Yes,' said the canon, 'a couple.'

'Good voices?'

'Quite.'

'How musical are you?' asked Harry.

'Only moderate, I'm afraid,' said the canon.

'Not as good as I am?'

'I don't know.'

'Well, I tell you, you're not as good as I am. I could have been a Mus. Doc. if I'd wanted to be.'

'I wouldn't put it past you,' said the canon.

'I've got perfect pitch,' said Harry.

'That's comparatively rare,' said the canon.

'Not as rare as you think,' said Harry. 'You haven't got it, I suppose?'

'No,' said the canon.

'I thought not,' said Harry. 'Then you can't be too sure how good your choir is.'

'I'm not an expert,' said the canon, 'but I can tell a good choir from a bad one.'

'But a couple of voices, you know, may spoil a good choir.'

'You mean two voices?' said the canon.

'Yes,' said Harry, 'I mean two. If I were you, I should tell them that their voices don't fit.'

'But they do,' said the canon.

'How do you know?' said Harry. 'You're not really a fit judge. I can tell better than you.'

'You haven't heard them sing yet,' said the canon.

'Oh yes, I have,' said Harry; 'they've sung privately to me. I've auditioned them, as you might say.'

'Don't you think they sing in tune?' asked the canon.

'It depends what tune,' said Harry. 'But they will be leaving the choir soon anyway, so there's not much point in keeping them, is there? After all, if they were good, you'd miss them when they went.'

'I can't tell them they've got bad voices when they haven't,' said the canon.

'You can't tell them anything else,' said Harry. 'If you give them no reason, they'll think that somebody must have told you that they've got bad voices. You've got neighbours too,' said Harry.

9 *Two Problems*

When the canon left Harry, he certainly had a problem. In one way he was elated. He knew that Harry was not a man to grass. He knew that it was absolutely against his nature. And yet, when it came to choosing between letting him run into danger and grassing, he chose the latter. Harry had plainly told him that two new members of the choir were out to escape and that personal violence was intended towards him. He had also advised him as strongly as he could that the way to deal with the situation was to get rid of the two men from the choir by pretending that their voices weren't good enough. This would have been a plain lie, and the canon simply could not tell it. On the other hand, if he simply removed them from the choir without giving any reasonable explanation they would realise that somebody had given them away. Whether or not they would know that the person concerned was Harry, at least that was a possibility. So the canon was in a very serious dilemma. He was not going to allow the men to escape, nor was he going to allow Harry to be beaten up. But how could he avoid both these contingencies? He thought about the matter for some time and eventually came to a conclusion.

The canon had two keys. One of them opened the chapel, and the other the classroom leading off it where choir practice was held. The obvious plan for men who wanted to escape was to choose choir practice, when they would have about an hour before their escape was discovered. The simplest plan was to take the keys off him and tie him up until they'd had sufficient time to make good their escape. Harry had indeed as good as told him that this was the plan. The canon did not think that he would die of fright, but he confessed to himself that he hoped that the men concerned did know how to gag a person without suffocating him.

In arriving at his own plan the canon had remembered something which Harry had said, namely that every good plan must be simple, and the canon's was. He adopted it whenever he went to choir practice. On the third occasion, after his interview with Harry, when choir practice took place, he had a feeling that this was the day. Accordingly he could not resist choosing as the first hymn to be practised 'Forth in Thy Name, O Lord, I Go'.

The canon's intuition was quite right. After five minutes of choir practice one of the two men approached him, and saying: 'Sorry, guv,' pinioned his arms behind his back. The other one then tied a handkerchief round his mouth and then put him on a chair to which they secured him. They then went through his pockets and extracted a key. This was the key of the classroom. But they looked in vain for the key of the chapel. The simple expedient adopted by the canon had been to leave that key behind and to ask a prison officer to open the chapel door at the end of choir practice. The result was that, though his assailants could get into the chapel, they could not get out of it. And their plan was a hopeless failure.

When they found that their plan had miscarried, the men undid the canon, locked the classroom door and gave him back the key. They also said that they were very sorry.

'Very well,' said the canon, 'we'll get on with the practice. I think we'll change the hymn to "Return, O Wanderer, to thy Home".'

The men sang it with a will.

Before the practice was over, the canon made an announcement.

'I do not propose,' he said, 'to make any report about this incident. I am taking this course for two reasons. First, because you showed no more than necessary violence towards me personally, for which I am extremely grateful. Secondly, because I want to give you an example, however feeble, of the fact that it is not necessary in this life to seek revenge. I don't pretend that I liked being gagged and bound. And it would have been natural if I had felt that I would get even with you. And it would have been easy to do so. But there is a great deal of good in all of us, even in me. And if I can do something like this, so can each of you. You can even get pleasure out of it, as I do from the knowledge that none of you will lose any remission for what you have done today. If you go through life trying to help people rather than hinder them, you will find you get very much more satisfaction. I don't mean you can do that always, there must be competition. And if two men are out for the same job, obviously they will each try to get it. Life is like that. But you will often get opportunities of helping your neighbour. We are all neighbours, one of another. Today I tried to help my neighbours. Tomorrow I hope you will do the same. As we have a few more minutes, we will sing the hymn "God Moves in a Mysterious Way His Wonders to Perform".'

A week later the canon went to see Harry again, and could tell from his face that the prison bush telegraph had been at work.

'Well done!' said Harry. 'We might go into partnership when I come out.'

'I've been suggesting that for some time,' said the canon.

'I hope you weren't roughed up too much,' said Harry.

'I'm quite all right,' said the canon, 'but I don't want to talk about it.'

'Well, I've got a real problem now,' said Harry.

'Oh, what's it this time? Nothing to do with the choir, I hope?'

'Oh lord, no. I've had a letter. Don't ask how I got it in.'

Harry handed it to the canon. It was written from Holloway prison.

'It's shaken me, I don't mind telling you,' said Harry. 'I only had three weeks with her, and now this. Read it.'

And the canon read:

My love,

I know you asked me not to write, and I said I wouldn't, but, when you see where I am, perhaps you won't mind so much. Now we're more or less in the same boat. It's a wonderful thing for me being in prison because I do feel that I'm with you. I don't suppose there's all that difference between men and women, and I try to picture you doing the things that I'm having to do. And when I'm by myself I feel that you're here too. Or that I'm in your cell with you. It's people that matter, not places. I could be happy with you in a dungeon. Where the light never came and the rats did. And then I think how wonderful it would be to be with you always – in the sunlight, in the fields, in London streets, on mountains and rivers, in the sea, on the sand, on the cliffs, at home in bed.

I wonder what you really think of me. I know that I was only an interlude. You told me so from the start. You warned me against getting fond of you. I did my best, really I did. But I couldn't help it. You are so kind. I wish love and kindness were the same thing, because then you must love me very much. But I know you don't, you were only your dear kind self.

May I come and meet you when you come out? I won't if you'd rather not, I'll disappear and never worry you again. I promise.

Sonia.

'Well,' said Harry, 'that's a bit of a teaser, isn't it?'

'D'you know what she's gone to prison for?' asked the canon.

'No idea at all.'

'Has she been there before?'

'Not to my knowledge.'

'If you ask me,' said the canon, 'I think she deliberately went to prison. She feels it's easier to wait for you in there than outside.'

'But she shouldn't be waiting for me at all,' said Harry. 'She admits it herself. You read that, didn't you?'

'Oh yes,' said the canon, 'I read that. It's easy for you to tell people not to care. But human beings just aren't like that.'

'We only knew each other for three weeks,' said Harry. 'I've had some of them for six months.'

'That was rather callous, wasn't it?' said the canon.

'I suppose so,' said Harry, 'but they can't have taken it too badly. None of them wrote to me. Until this one. What do I do about it?'

'Did you like her?' asked the canon.

'Of course I liked her,' said Harry. 'I'd only got a few weeks. I wasn't going to have somebody I didn't like.'

'Yes,' said the canon, 'but, until you live with a person, you can't really tell.'

'How do you know?' asked Harry. 'How many people have you lived with?'

'Fair comment,' said the canon. 'But did you like her more than any of the others?'

'I can't say that I did,' said Harry. 'But certainly not less. She's a nice girl, I grant you.' He thought for a few moments. 'Yes, on the whole,' he said, 'she's the sort of girl I oughtn't to see for more than a few weeks. I might have got too fond of her. But perhaps it's that letter. It's got under my skin, I suppose. I'll have to write to her, won't I?'

'That's up to you,' said the canon. 'But, if she's a really nice girl, I wish you'd get married to her. She'd be the saving of you.'

'Perhaps I don't want to be saved,' said Harry.

'We've been into all this before.'

'That's what worries me. I feel I've got to write back. It would be like hitting a child not to. But then she'll write back to me and I'll write back to her and so on. And, if it goes on like this until I come out, how can I tell her not to meet me? I'm scared stiff, I can tell you.'

'Good,' said the canon. 'Would you like me to go and see her when I go to London?'

'If you'd promise to put her off me,' said Harry, 'I most certainly would.'

'You know perfectly well,' said the canon, 'that I should do nothing of the kind. In fact I warn you that, if I think she's a suitable wife for you, I shall do everything I can to get you married to her.'

'I thought you were a friend,' said Harry.

'You know I am.'

'I don't want to get married. I'm very happy as I am. I've told you before. If I get married, it'll change my whole way of life. I make a success of this way. Heaven knows what I'd do with another.'

'A success you call it?' said the canon.

'Of course I do,' said Harry. 'I bet you couldn't do as well. Would they have me in the church, d'you think?'

'You are in the church,' said the canon.

'You know what I mean,' said Harry. 'Would they let me be ordained? It's only theoretical, I assure you. But would they have a chap with eight previous convictions? Or is it nine, I forget. If they were satisfied that I'd really repented?'

'There would be difficulties,' said the canon. 'For one thing there could only be one human being who would know if you really had repented. And that would be you. On the whole I think the authorities would say it would be too much of a risk to take.'

'I'm glad I wasn't serious,' said Harry.

'Well,' said the canon, 'unless you ask me not to do so, I shall go and call on Sonia when I next get the chance in London.'

'If you do that,' said Harry, 'you might find out what she's in for.'

'Why should you want to know that?' asked the canon.

'Curiosity,' said Harry. 'She didn't strike me as the sort of girl who'd steal or anything like that.'

'Perhaps she caught it from you,' said the canon.

'I don't normally steal,' said Harry, 'but I suppose it's very much the same thing. Yes, I might have given her the idea. But she obviously wasn't much good at it. I wonder how many offences she's committed because normally they can't be sent to gaol for a first offence. Perhaps she has a record after all. I never asked her.'

'I tell you,' said the canon, 'I believe she did something quite deliberately in order to get sent to prison. I strongly suspect that she forced the magistrate to send her to prison by refusing to be put on probation or refusing to agree to the other terms he may have offered her for a discharge. She wants to share your life, Harry. And while you're in prison that's the nearest she can get to it.'

'Well,' said Harry, 'if my wife were sent to prison, I shouldn't go to gaol just to show how much I loved her, I assure you. Who'd look after the home?'

'She isn't your wife,' said the canon. 'Not yet anyway.'

'And what a life it would be,' said Harry. 'I'd be in gaol

most of the time. I'm not coming out while that so-and-so's still abroad.'

'Abroad,' repeated the canon. 'That's an idea. Why don't you marry her and go and settle in Australia or somewhere? There you'd be safe.'

'That's what you say,' said Harry. 'I shouldn't be safe anywhere in the world from that fellow. Not in the north pole or the south pole, or in a submarine. He'd find me. I don't blame him either. If you'd ever had sixty thousand quid nicked off you, you'd want to find the chap, wouldn't you? Anyway you're different, it isn't the same thing. I'm damned certain that there's nowhere in the world I shall be safe so long as that chap's at large. And I'm not taking any chances.'

'Even if he's not caught for twenty years or more?' said the canon.

'As long as he's not caught full stop,' said Harry.

'It's an awful waste,' said the canon.

'That's as may be,' said Harry. 'But I know a safe place when I see one, and this is the place for me until they get the fellow.'

'Why don't you find out where he is,' said the canon, 'and give the police a tip-off? There are sure to be people in the underworld who know.'

'Be your age,' said Harry. 'My principles aren't as good as yours, but I've got them all the same. I wouldn't tip off the police to catch a murderer.'

'A murderer of children?' queried the canon.

'Oh, stop it,' said Harry. 'There's always an exceptional case.'

'A blackmailer, then?' queried the canon.

'I shouldn't think so,' said Harry. 'Most of us stick to the rules, and although it's true I am frightened of being beaten up, that isn't the reason in this case. I'd never give a chap away, whatever he'd done, unless there were quite exceptional circumstances. Children, I grant you, might be different. And there could be others, of course. But normally the answer's No, and I certainly wouldn't do it to save my own skin. Not because I'm not frightened, you know I am, frightened as hell. I suppose I'm one of the biggest cowards in the business. Otherwise you wouldn't get me spending years in prison. But we are all made differently, and that's how I am. You're the same in a sense. Truth's your bug. But you'll find there's an exception even to that.'

'No,' said the canon, 'I won't admit that.'

'Of course you won't admit it, you hope there won't be. But one day you'll find something happens which makes you tell a lie. And a real one, I mean. Not one of those half-truths which some people like using in order to skate round lies.'

'I think they're worse than lies,' said the canon. 'You're deceiving the other person just as you intend, but pretending to yourself that you haven't told a lie. So, in point of fact, there are two sins there. Both lying and hypocrisy. But there are a large number of people who do it.'

'And some of them,' said Harry, 'I can sympathise with. Doctors, for example. They'll skate round the truth if they can, in the interests of their patient. Who can blame them?'

'I can,' said the canon, 'and I do. Anyway what are you going to do about Sonia's letter?'

Harry sighed. 'I shall have to answer it,' he said, 'but don't ask me how I'll get the letter out. I won't ask you to take it.'

10 *Answer from a Long Firm*

The same day Harry answered Sonia's letter.

Sonia dear, he wrote, *I loved your letter. But what on earth are you doing in Holloway? Don't tell me I taught you. It's no place for a girl like you. D'you realise you're one of seven hundred? Women are so good, there are only about a thousand of them in prison. There are thirty thousand or more of us. You've said before that you'd do whatever I wanted. Please don't do this again. I hate to think of you all cooped up. You make me think of all the lovely things that I enjoy when I'm out.*

But I didn't start out to say this. What I meant to say is that I'm no good to you – no good at all. I'm selfish and idle. What's the good of that to a woman? Well, there are lots of other selfish and idle men around, I know that, and there are plenty of women living with or married to them. And most of them aren't always in and out of gaol as I am. Most men are selfish, I suppose. But not many are as idle as I am. And I enjoy cheating people. Oddly enough, I haven't told you *any lies, but if there were any need to, I certainly would. Nothing really means anything to me, except* me. *I live for myself. All right, I was nice to you. That was easy enough. You were nice to me. I got what I wanted by being nice to you. And I must say, it's easier to be nice to a sweet girl like you than to be the other thing.*

You should be married to a decent solid civil servant – someone who'll leave the house at half past eight and come back at six and never give you a moment's anxiety. When I *left the house you'd never know whether I was coming back or not. And how would you feel when the police started coming round and making enquiries? And not such polite enquiries either.*

I'm not really a man any decent girl should have anything to do with, even if she has *been in Holloway. D'you know what one judge once said to me: 'I try a lot of criminals,' he said, 'and I'm sorry for some of them. They've no trade, no skills, no education. And there's precious little remunerative work they can do. But you, you're an educated man of considerable ability and you could earn an honest living if you wanted to. The trouble is, you prefer to prey on the public. You could be of great use to the country. Instead of which you're a minus quantity. You live by robbing and cheating. And from what you've said to me, I don't detect the slightest suggestion that you propose to change your mode of life in the future.' 'My Lord,' I said, 'if there had been, you wouldn't have believed it.' 'Don't be insolent,' he said. Of course, if I had said that I was sorry, that I'd go straight in the future, that I'd learned my lesson and that I wanted to live an honest life, he'd probably have said: 'You're only sorry because you're caught. You've been living on the proceeds of crime for years and years. And now you ask me to believe that you're proposing to turn over a new leaf. Well, it's no use saying I do. I don't!'*

Anyway, it doesn't make any difference what they say because the sentence is going to be the same. There was only one time earlier on, when a judge didn't send me to prison at all. And then he laid it on thicker than ever, before telling me I could go. I suppose that was to give me a good fright. I'm afraid he didn't succeed.

I shouldn't make fun of judges, should I? They're not too bad on the whole, and they've got a job to do. I shouldn't like it.

I shouldn't like to be a member of parliament, either. I shouldn't like to do anything with responsibility. All I want is freedom. 'That's a funny thing to say,' you'll say, 'writing from prison.' But, believe me, I'm a damn sight freer here than a lot of people outside. And I'm safe too. No one comes to arrest me here. The rules and regulations in a prison are nothing to those outside. But it isn't a place for a girl – not a girl like you, anyway. So don't do it again, please. Anyway, I don't know what you did. It must have been pretty bad to land you in Holloway. It's still a man's world, so we don't send women to prison more often than we can help. We like them outside to look beautiful and comfort us. What's the good of a woman in prison?

This isn't at all the letter that I meant to write. I'm just talking to you as I did when we were together. And I must admit I like it. That's me all over – just thinking of myself. But thinking of myself, if you are around when I come out, I'd love to meet you again. But I warn you, you'll be sorry. You'll be hurt – I know it. So if you're sensible, you'll clear off. I shall be sorry, I'll admit, but I'll understand. I oughtn't really to have answered your letter at all. If I hadn't been as selfish as I am, I shouldn't have.

Oh, by the way, if ever you're in trouble, I've got a friend who can help. He's a parson, but don't mind that. He's a really good fellow. Don't tell him any lies. He's trying to make a good man out of me, poor chap. And I must say he's trying very hard. But he hasn't a hope. I've told him so no end of times. That doesn't make the slightest difference. Back he comes for more. I knocked him down once. He was a bit hurt after that, but he soon forgave and forgot. I must say, I didn't like doing it. I hate violence, even my own. You're lucky there. I shouldn't ever knock you about. But don't you knock me about either. What a lot of nonsense I'm talking. And I suppose it's all because I like you a bit too much.

Harry.

In a P.S. he sent Sonia Canon Abdale's address.

Harry was not surprised that he got a letter in reply.

My dear, she wrote,

I've read your letter six times and I shall read it sixty times more. How sweet and good you are. Don't worry about me at all. I shall never get in your way. If I can just see you from time to time, that will be heaven. I promise I'll never be a bore, or a menace. I'll go right away whenever you want me to. What a wonderful thought to think I shall be with you again some time. I never really thought you'd let me. It's been a new life to me to know you. I don't mind what you've done or what you'll do. You're someone who will always be with me, whatever happens. Even if I never saw you again, you'd always be with me. Always and always.

Your letter has really made me quite light-headed. I walked round and round my cell saying: 'I'm going to see him again, I'm going to see him again.' Your parson friend should be pleased. I said 'Hallelujah!' at the end. But, to tell you the truth, I'm not quite sure what it means. But it's thanking somebody for something. You're quite right about freedom. I'm free as air here – ever since I got your letter, that is. I'm thinking of you all the time. What a silly man that judge was; but then I suppose they have to say things like that.

There's so much I want to say to you. I seem to think the same way you do. It's so awful when you talk to a person and they can't understand anything you say. I was brought up with a sister who was like that. We might have been speaking a foreign language to each other. But she never went to Holloway. As a matter of fact, she married a stockbroker – couldn't be more respectable than that. All right; I won't do it again, if you don't want me to. I shall be out in a few weeks. It was only shoplifting and I got in by refusing to pay the fine.

How long will it be before I see you? And where shall we meet, and where shall we go? Can I come and meet you on the day you come out? Or would you hate that? I shan't sleep at all tonight. I'm so excited. I keep on saying to myself, 'He's written to me, he's written to me!' I never thought you would. I wanted you to so badly. But don't be unkind to yourself to be kind to me. I'm sure I shall feel it if I'm only a nuisance, and you won't have to tell me to go. I shall just drop off. That isn't true. You will *have to tell me. I couldn't bear the idea that I might be wrong, and go, when after all you wanted me to stay. But you won't have to tell me twice, I promise. Really you won't. Just say you've had enough of me and I shall be gone. Now I'm being morbid. You make me so happy that I can't think of ever being unhappy again. Oh, thank you, thank you, thank you. Sleep well, dear one.*

Sonia.

11 *Stephen Stratford*

While Harry was corresponding with Sonia and the canon was hoping that one day he would have the pleasure of marrying them, the man of whom Harry was very reasonably afraid was waiting anxiously for Harry's release. Like Harry, he had none of the usual excuses for being a criminal, but unlike Harry, he was certainly not a kind person. He had never been kind. From birth he had tormented his parents, and from the time when he had begun first ill-treating animals and then bullying smaller boys, he had been thoroughly vicious. It is difficult if not impossible to explain why the Almighty creates people with this seed of vice in them. It seems to be rather bad luck on those who are doomed from the start. Another not very profitable field of enquiry is to consider whether the Almighty watches his creatures move from place to place and cross each other's paths. Does he have a map like a general with pins stuck in to represent the different parties? And does he view with compassion, interest or amusement the movement of two human beings towards each other, knowing that, when they meet, there will be a head-on collision or an explosion of some kind?

The man's name was Stephen Stratford. He had organised the raid on the bank with skill, efficiency and ruthlessness. He had no particular wish to kill or wound bank-clerks or passers-by, but if, in the course of his business, it was necessary to mow them down, mown down they would certainly be. Two bank-clerks and one passer-by did get in the way. They were shot, but not killed. Three others were shot at, but were not hit. It is in fact extremely difficult for anyone except an expert to hit a person with a revolver bullet, even at quite close range, and there are very few shots in the world who could be sure of killing a man with one shot only.

After the raid, they all escaped, but a disgruntled member of the gang, who thought he hadn't been promised enough of the swag, gave information which led to the arrest of Stephen Stratford. Shortly before he was caught Stephen had learned of the danger of arrest and that was how he came to give the money hurriedly to Harry.

Not long after his escape from prison he went abroad and then he started to make enquiries to see where Harry was. When he found out that he was in prison, he used the recognised means of communication and tried to get in touch with Harry. He was alarmed to find that he could get no reply. He tried again, and yet again, but always without success. He did not believe for a moment that Harry was unaware of his efforts to get in touch with him. For the expert criminal who knows all about prisons, it is almost as easy to communicate with and from a prison as it is to post a letter through the Post Office. It is, of course, pretty expensive, but as postal rates go up, soon there may not be very much in it. Stephen assumed from his getting no satisfactory answers from Harry that he had made away with the money, or at any rate was not prepared to give it back to him. It was not surprising that he was angry. He had taken all the time and trouble and risk to collect sixty thousand pounds, and now another man, who had done nothing whatever towards the collection of the money, was going to reap the benefit of it all or had already done so. At this point Stephen, strangely enough, had something in common with the Almighty who, it will be remembered, said in his infinite mercy: 'Vengeance is mine.'

When Harry's term was drawing to its close Stephen came back to England. But he had to be extremely careful. He was not much freer than Harry was. He did not venture into the streets by day or by night, but stayed in one room, where, as far as anything in this world can be certain, he knew he was safe. He was sufficiently supplied with food to be able to live, and in that one room he lived and waited. And, as he waited, he spent much of his time thinking of his meeting with Harry. Perhaps all the money had not been spent, and there would be some left. But the one thing he promised himself was that after that meeting there would be nothing left of Harry. Unless he was wrong in thinking that Harry had used the money or some of it for himself. If he *was* wrong, then he would be very happy to forgo his vengeance in exchange for the pleasure which sixty thousand precious pounds would give him.

Revenge was part of Stephen's make-up. He was one of the few criminals who had really contemplated revenge upon a judge. It is perhaps surprising that such revenge is seldom contemplated and never effected in this country. To a man sentenced to a long period of imprisonment, however justly, the robed figure, cool and calculating, sitting above him must sometimes become an object of hatred, particularly when the figure gives tongue. Some people question whether a judge should ever address the prisoner before sentencing him. But, while it is normally desirable in the interests of common humanity that the sentence should precede any homily, it must sometimes be necessary in the public interest that the reasons for the sentence should be stated. Otherwise, the fact that prisoner A gets five years and prisoner B fifty might upset the public. Quite a substantial proportion of the public, who would think very differently if their own home were invaded and their own property taken, seem to have a sneaking sympathy with those who rob banks or large institutions. And the sympathy is not always so sneaking. A good many people today have sympathy with members of the gang who participated in the Great Train Robbery. They seem to forget that one man was badly injured in that affair and that others might have been if they had shown resistance. They seem to have a kind of envious admiration of the person or persons who devised the scheme, and almost a regret that they were not able to get away with the proceeds. But someone did get away with the proceeds. Only about ten per cent – which is now smaller than the gratuity given to many waiters – was left behind.

Stephen had undoubtedly contemplated revenge and had very nearly put into effect his deep hatred of the judge who had sentenced him. He made no secret of his feelings to his friends. 'Thin-lipped bastard,' he had said, 'I'd like to sentence him.' The judge, in fact, was a most compassionate man and disliked taking criminal cases for the very reason that he had to sentence people. But it was undoubtedly difficult for Stephen at the wrong end of a sentence of thirty years' imprisonment to appreciate the judge's feelings, even if he had been told about them. 'You were the organiser of this robbery,' said Mr Justice Grainger to him. 'You showed no mercy to those who got in your way and I should be failing in my duty to the public if I showed any mercy towards you. Should another court, or the Home Secretary, think the sentence which I am about to impose upon you is too long, they can alter it. But the public must be protected from violent robbers.'

After Stephen had escaped he did not immediately go abroad. He in fact found Mr Justice Grainger and followed him along the Embankment as he walked away from another day's work at the Old Bailey. Stephen had a loaded revolver with him and was walking immediately behind the judge, who was wholly unaware of his presence. As the two walked along the Embankment, the judge about ten yards in front of Stephen, no one recognised either of them. No one realised that the man behind was visualising himself walking straight up to the judge, putting his revolver in his back and giving him just enough time to have a split second of fear before pulling the trigger – once, twice, however many times might be necessary. He did it in his imagination and it was very pleasant. He would have liked to have given him more than the split second of fear, but that would have been too dangerous. The judge might have turned round and struggled, and in the struggle Stephen might have missed. If Stephen shot at him from a distance, he might easily miss. But there would be no difficulty in getting right up to the judge and putting the revolver in the small of his back. Three pulls at the trigger would surely kill him.

As Stephen walked along he recalled the scene when he had been sentenced. He saw the face of the judge, with his mouth opening and shutting as he pronounced sentence. 'The thin-lipped bastard,' he said again to himself. Twice he nearly ran forward and did it. He was not prevented by any twinges of conscience. If he could have done it and made sure of his escape, he would have unquestionably shot the judge, but each time the difficulties of escape seemed too great. There were too many people about, and, though he could shoot his way through some of them, the chances of his making a get-away were small. He looked at the people as they walked along. Every twenty yards or so the scene varied slightly. He looked for his best corridor of escape. They never passed a policeman, but that is hardly surprising. On the beat they seem few and far between. If he were to be caught, he would probably get a life sentence or another thirty years, or heaven knows what. He would certainly never come out of prison, except by escaping; and it would be most unlikely that he would be allowed to escape twice, even with his influence inside a prison.

If the Almighty had been looking on at that moment, it is difficult to imagine that he would not have been affected by the scene. But it has to be remembered that the Almighty is probably not like the audience at a cinema, or the reader of a novel. The audience or the reader would know that the judge was thinking about some abstruse question of law, or about his grandchildren, or about the port which he had drunk the night before, wholly unaware that death was stalking him. The audience or the reader would be saying: 'Will he, won't he? Will he, won't he?', some of them hoping he would and some of them hoping he wouldn't.

From time to time on their walk the public thinned out and it was then that the judge came closest to death. 'I could get up that street,' Stephen said to himself, 'before the public realised what had happened. And round the corner, I could start walking as though nothing had occurred. No one would recognise me.' But before he had taken advantage of the situation, they had walked on, and now there were more people, and there was no turning available for his escape. Stephen had taken a lot of trouble, and spent quite a lot of money in escaping from prison. Eventually, he came to the conclusion that it would be madness to risk losing everything for what would be a moment's satisfaction. No, it would be more than a moment, because he would be able to think about it again and again. But it would be one thing to think about it in freedom in South America, quite another to think about it in a cell in an English prison. He finally decided that he must be satisfied with the recollection of what *might* have been. In the end he walked right up to the judge, to within one foot of him, visualised what could have happened, and then abruptly turned to the right and abandoned the idea. The judge continued to think peacefully about a word in a crossword puzzle which had eluded him, and which he had been trying to get ever since he left the steps of the Old Bailey. The clue was: 'Two donkeys, one without a tail, lead to sin'. The coincidence of the word to which this was the clue should enable many crossword-solvers to find it.

Having left Mr Justice Grainger alive, Stephen went swiftly to Portugal. He could speak several languages including Portuguese, and he had already established himself in a house in a village in Portugal under a different name and with a different passport. No one there connected him with various large robberies which had taken place in England. It's a sensible thing to have your home many hundred miles from the scene of your crimes. Although fast air travel has existed for a long time now, it is still a little difficult for people to visualise the respectable Englishman whom they have seen walking along the village street three days previously, as the leading spirit in a big bullion raid in London two days later. Owing to his arrest, he was detained in England rather longer than he had anticipated, but this made no difference to his reputation in the Portuguese village. Naturally, an Englishman will want to go to England from time to time, and how long he stays there is his business.

Stephen had put his ability in languages to good use during the war. He became an interpreter. And, as this involved his association with criminals, some of whom had some money, he found it quite a lucrative position. Moreover, it kept him a long way away from the fighting. He even carried on with the work of an interpreter for a short time after the war was over. But the money was insufficient and so he gave up interpreting and went back to crime in a big way. He was very successful. All his plans were carefully worked out and the people he used to carry them out were encouraged by him to do what he told them. They were paid really well, but if they didn't toe the line, they were beaten up or murdered, or both.

He was only caught twice. It was on the first occasion that he met Harry in prison. But he didn't have to escape then, because a mistake had been made by the judge at his trial and he was acquitted in the Court of Appeal. It was just before he was caught on the second occasion that he made his big mistake in trusting Harry. He knew that Harry must have learned of his reputation, and felt confident that an ordinary con man wouldn't dare to let him down. There were too many examples of the consequences of letting Stephen Stratford down known to the criminal world. He did not realise that money in Harry's hands was money to be spent, whatever the consequences might be.

Having regard to Harry's failure to answer any of his communications, Stephen felt more or less sure that the money was not intact. If his forebodings were correct, he had no doubt what he was going to do. The judge and Harry were two very different cases. To have killed the judge would have given him some satisfaction but would have produced nothing else. To kill Harry was almost a necessity. It was vital that the criminal world should know that you couldn't get away with it if you double-crossed Stephen. No one would learn a lesson from his having killed the judge. The next judge to try him would try him just as fairly or unfairly irrespective of the fate of Mr Justice Grainger. The next man to whom he handed sixty thousand pounds would be pretty careful to hand them back again, if he knew of Harry's fate. It was true that he would be carrying on his activities mainly from abroad, but nevertheless he did not propose to go out of business just because he was an escaped prisoner. So he waited as patiently as he could for news of Harry's release.

12 *Defence in Depth*

When he was released Harry went straight to the colonel's flat and finding that he was away he brought Sonia there, and they made themselves very much at home. The same evening they discussed his future movements.

'I've got to get back to prison,' he said. 'If I don't, sooner or later, Stratford or one of his thugs will find me and then I shall be for it. And I don't want to be for it. And you don't want me to be for it.'

'I certainly don't,' said Sonia.

'Well, I've no alternative,' said Harry. 'Now what's it to be?'

'I don't mind what it is,' said Sonia, 'so long as I'm in it with you.'

'Certainly not,' said Harry. 'That's one thing I insist upon. I'm not having you involved. I don't mind telling you what I'm doing, because nobody will know that I've told you. But I'm not going to have you picked up with me.'

'Whatever you say,' said Sonia, 'but I'd love to help.'

'Now, let me think,' said Harry. 'As I've often said, the simplest ideas are always the best. What I want is a nice simple crime with a complete defence, which I can raise if necessary but which no one will know about, unless I do in fact raise it.' He thought for a few minutes.

'Good gracious,' he said eventually. 'I wonder why I've

never thought of this before. It's really too simple. We're going to see a solicitor.'

'But surely a solicitor won't want to involve himself in a crime,' said Sonia.

'Of course not,' said Harry. 'I'm not going to ask him to. I'm just going to ask him to witness something. He won't know who I am, as I shall use a different name. And, if eventually I'm charged with the crime, he won't identify either the crime or the criminal with me. But, if I should suddenly want to show that I'm innocent, I shall have the perfect witness.'

'Well, I'm sure you know what you're doing,' said Sonia, 'but at present I don't understand.'

'Of course you don't,' said Harry. 'Nor would anyone else. But come along to the solicitor and then you'll see. Now who shall we go to? Let's walk along Piccadilly and choose a likely name.'

They went out and walked along the street. Eventually they came to a block of offices and they looked at the names.

'Ah, this will do nicely – Messrs Longmore, Creavley & Stamp,' read out Harry. 'I wonder if there is a Longmore, a Creavley or a Stamp. It's probably all run by a gentleman called Higgins. Come along, then. We'll go and see Mr Higgins.'

They took the lift and eventually entered the offices of Messrs Longmore, Creavley & Stamp. They were shown into a waiting room.

'Have you an appointment?' asked the girl receptionist.

'No, I'm afraid not,' said Harry. 'I won't keep anybody very long, but I should like to see a partner.'

'Who would you like to see?' asked the girl. 'Mr Longmore, Mr Creavley or Mr Stamp?'

'Good gracious!' said Harry.

'I beg your pardon?' said the girl.

'Nothing,' said Harry. 'I'm so sorry. I was surprised at being offered such a choice without notice.'

'I didn't say they'd be available,' said the girl. 'I just wanted to know who you'd like to see.'

Harry thought for a moment. 'The one with the best memory, please.'

'That's an odd thing to say,' said the girl.

'I don't know why,' said Harry. 'He's never seen me before and I want him to remember me.'

'Well,' said the girl, 'Mr Longmore's the youngest, so I suppose he'd have the best memory.'

'The senior partner, the youngest?' queried Harry.

'Certainly not,' said the girl. 'Mr Longmore's dead.'

'Oh, I see,' said Harry. 'This is his son.'

'No,' said the girl, 'Mr Longmore's son is also dead. The present Mr Longmore is the great-great-grandson of the founder of the firm.'

'What about Mr Creavley?' said Harry. 'Is he dead, too?'

'This is Mr Creavley, junior. He doesn't usually come to the office any more. But he happens to be here today. Somehow I don't think he'd suit your purpose. He's ninety-five.'

'Wonderful old man,' said Harry.

'He is,' said the girl. 'His brain's quicker than mine.'

'What about Mr Stamp,' said Harry, 'is he nearly a centenarian too?'

'Oh, no,' said the girl, 'he's quite young. He's just on eighty.'

'Just a moment,' said Harry. 'Would you mind telling me how old Mr Longmore is? I mean the present Mr Longmore.'

'Really,' said the girl. 'I've never had a client so inquisitive before.'

'I do apologise,' said Harry, 'but my business is rather important and, as I said when I came in, I do want somebody with a good memory.'

'Both Mr Creavley and Mr Stamp have excellent memories,' said the girl.

'I take your word for it,' said Harry, 'but however good their memories are, they won't be any use to me if they're dead. Now, I hope they'll both live for many, many years, but you can't deny that at the age of eighty and ninety-five there is at least the possibility that they won't be alive in a couple of months' time.'

'You may not be,' said the girl.

'True,' said Harry, 'but I can skip out of the way of cars more quickly than Mr Creavley or Mr Stamp, I should think.'

'You haven't seen them,' said the girl. 'How can you tell? They skip very quickly indeed. In fact Mr Stamp brought an action a little while ago against a cyclist who knocked him down.'

'Apparently, then,' said Harry, 'he didn't skip quickly enough.'

'This was on the pavement,' said the girl. 'You don't expect to have to skip on the pavement.'

'Well, I'm glad it was Mr Stamp and not Mr Creavley. I don't imagine Mr Creavley would respond well to being knocked down.'

'He responds excellently,' said the girl. 'He was knocked down by a car.'

'Well, then, *he* must have failed to skip,' said Harry.

'Not a bit. It was in his own front door. A car came right into the front door just as Mr Creavley was coming out. If he hadn't been so thin, he might have been badly hurt. Now, if you've finished asking me questions, I'll go and see if Mr Longmore can see you. Can you tell me what it's about?'

'Yes,' said Harry, 'I want him to witness something.'

'A will?'

'No, not a will. Much simpler than a will.'

'Very well, then,' said the girl. 'Please sit down. I won't keep you waiting for longer than is necessary.'

Ten minutes later, they were shown into Mr Longmore's office. Harry was pleased to see that he was about forty to fifty.

'Well,' said Mr Longmore, 'where's the affidavit?'

'There isn't an affidavit,' said Harry.

'I thought you'd come to swear one.'

'No, I haven't come to swear at all.'

'Miss Higgins distinctly told me it was an affidavit.'

'Did you say Higgins?' said Harry.

'Yes,' said Mr Longmore, 'Miss Higgins, the receptionist.'

'How odd,' said Harry.

'I don't see that there's anything odd about it,' said Mr Longmore, 'but even if there is, I'm afraid I don't want to discuss it. Will you kindly state your business. But first please, your name?'

'My name is Arbuthnot,' said Harry. 'Harry Arbuthnot. And my address is Q5, Albany, Piccadilly.'

Mr Longmore did not actually get up, but it was obvious that the mention of Albany raised his opinion of Harry immediately.

'Very well, Mr Arbuthnot,' he said in more genial tones than he had previously used. 'What can I have the pleasure of doing for you?'

'I have here a five pound note,' said Harry, 'I'd be grateful if you'd make a note of the number.'

Mr Longmore did so.

'And here I have a registered letter addressed to the British Universal Stores Limited at their head office. I shall be very grateful if you will insert the one in the other and post it personally.'

'That's a rather odd request, Mr Arbuthnot,' said Mr Longmore. 'Conscience money?'

'You're not suggesting, I hope,' said Harry, 'in the presence of my friend (who is also called Higgins), that I've been stealing from one of the multiple stores owned by Messrs British Universal Stores Limited?'

'I'm not suggesting anything,' said Mr Longmore. 'I merely said it was an odd request.'

'But you added,' said Harry, 'with an enquiry in your voice, you added "conscience money". How can conscience money be due unless I've done something to weigh heavily upon my conscience – or if not heavily, at any rate, to weigh upon it – and why should my conscience be weighed upon if I have not stolen from one of the stores?'

'You're not bound to tell me your business if you don't want to,' said Mr Longmore. 'But at the moment I can't think why anyone should want to send five pounds for nothing to British Universal Stores Limited.'

'I can only assure you,' said Harry, 'that I have stolen nothing from British Universal Stores Limited, or from anybody else, as a matter of fact.'

Mr Longmore thought for a moment.

'Well, I can't see anything wrong in sending them five pounds. Don't you want your name, or any note put in with it?'

'No, thank you,' said Harry. 'Just the money. If you are at all doubtful as to whether you ought to do it, Mr Longmore, why don't you consult with your partners? I'd love to meet them and I'm quite prepared to pay the additional fee.'

Mr Longmore got up. 'Mr Arbuthnot,' he said. 'I don't know what your object is in coming here, but I'm afraid I am not prepared to do what you ask. Good morning. There will be no charge.'

'Well, if that's how you feel . . .' began Harry.

'That is exactly how I feel,' said Mr Longmore.

'Could you by any chance recommend another firm?' asked Harry.

'No,' said Mr Longmore, 'I could not. Most solicitors are responsible people and are not prepared to be driven in blinkers.'

'I must say,' said Harry, 'the thought of you and Mr Creavley and Mr Stamp in blinkers is a very happy one. And on that happy note, I bid you good morning, Mr Longmore. Come along, Miss Higgins.'

As they left the outer office Harry could not resist saying to the girl:

'I'd no idea your name was Higgins.'

'It isn't,' said the girl. 'That was the last one. She married Mr Creavley. I've only been here a fortnight, so sometimes they make a mistake.'

'It was Mr Longmore who said it,' said Harry, 'the one with the good memory.'

'I didn't say he had a good memory,' said the girl. 'I said he had the best memory. Good morning.'

They left the office and were soon in Piccadilly.

'Now you understand,' said Harry.

'I'm afraid I don't,' said Sonia. 'I'm sure you haven't been pinching things from shops.'

'No,' said Harry, 'but I'm going to.'

'I don't follow,' said Sonia, 'they only fine people for doing that.'

'Oh,' said Harry, 'that's on a first or second or third occasion. I'm an old hand. With my record they'd send me for sentence to sessions. So you follow now?'

'I'm not quite sure,' said Sonia.

'Well, it's quite simple,' said Harry. 'First of all I put myself in a position to prove conclusively that I've sent five pounds to the British Universal Stores. Then I take goods to the value of something less than five pounds. I'm duly found out, arrested and charged, and if I still want to go to prison, off I go. If, on the other hand, they should catch Mr Stratford, I've got a cast-iron defence. I can prove that I paid for the goods in advance.'

'Why don't you try and find out where he is,' said Sonia, 'and then tell the police?'

'My dear girl,' said Harry, 'you don't understand my principles. I've got a lot of them, you know. I wouldn't turn anybody over to the police.'

'Not even if he were going to kill you?'

'No,' said Harry, 'not even if he were going to kill me. And after all I can sympathise with him. Now, where shall we go?' They came to another set of offices. 'Ah, this looks quite promising. Mr Peter Broadwas, Solicitor and Commissioner for Oaths. I can see that I shall have to tell more of a story, or they may not do what I ask.'

Ten minutes later they were in the office of Mr Broadwas.

'It's a rather delicate matter,' explained Harry. 'My name is Arbuthnot, and my address is Q5, Albany, Piccadilly. I have a young nephew whose name is – well, perhaps, if it isn't essential, I'd rather not give you his name for the moment.'

'Until I know what your business is, Mr Arbuthnot,' said Mr Broadwas, 'I can't tell whether I must know the name of your nephew.'

'The position is this,' said Harry. 'My nephew went on a shoplifting spree and he confined his activities to one of the stores of British Universal Stores Limited.'

'Has he been charged?' asked Mr Broadwas.

'No,' said Harry, 'they never caught him. But he told me about it. He stole goods to the value of £4 16*s*. 11*d*. If he took them back, they might charge him. So what I want to do is to send them this five pound note, and I want to be able to prove that I have sent it.'

'I see,' said Mr Broadwas.

'The point,' said Harry, 'is this. Although I don't think it's likely for one moment that they will ever discover that my nephew was responsible for the theft, there is always the one chance in ten thousand that this may happen. At least I want the goods to have been paid for if he is charged. But apart from that, I do want the goods to have been paid for, and if you'll be good enough to send this five pounds for me, they *will* have been paid for. I don't want to disclose my own name, or they'll obviously come and ask me questions about it. And I certainly don't propose to give my nephew's name.'

'It's really a case of conscience money,' said Mr Broadwas.

'Exactly,' said Harry; 'you couldn't have put it better. And if you will be kind enough to take this five pound note, put it in this registered envelope and post it yourself, personally, having first taken the number of the note, I shall sleep much better. First of all I shall know that British Universal Stores have been recompensed for my nephew's theft; secondly, I shall know that, whatever happens, I can prove conclusively through you, sir, that the money has been paid to them. Very likely in those circumstances they wouldn't even prosecute, even if they did find out.'

'That certainly is quite possible,' said Mr Broadwas.

'Are you prepared to undertake this service for me?' said Harry.

'I don't see why not,' said Mr Broadwas. 'It's a perfectly proper thing to do. There's no question of compounding a felony or anything of that sort. Yes, Mr Arbuthnot, I'm perfectly prepared to do this for you.'

'And your fee?' said Harry.

'My fee?' said Mr Broadwas, 'Well, there's nothing to it really. If I charge you a nominal guinea, will that be all right?'

'Most certainly,' said Harry, 'and I'm most grateful to you.'

Mr Broadwas started to write out a receipt and Harry got out one pound, one shilling. Suddenly, Harry said:

'Forgive me, Mr Broadwas, but haven't we met before somewhere?' Mr Broadwas looked at Harry.

'I don't think so,' he said. 'Where do you think we may have met?'

'I know,' said Harry. 'By the lion cage in the Zoo. A man nearly had his hand bitten off by a lion and got ticked off by one of the keepers. We had a chat about it.'

'No,' said Mr Broadwas, 'I'm afraid it was somebody else.'

'Forgive my asking, but do you go to the Zoo at all, Mr Broadwas?'

'No,' said Mr Broadwas, 'I have *never* been to the Zoo.'

'It follows from that,' said Harry, 'that you don't know the lions' cage.'

'That is a logical deduction,' said Mr Broadwas. 'Here is your receipt, and I will post the letter today myself. Would you like me to keep the registered receipt, or shall I send it on to you?'

'No, please keep it,' said Harry. 'Please keep it in your safe, so that it always will be available.'

'Be it so,' said Mr Broadwas.

Sonia and Harry left the building and strolled into St James's Park.

'I'm afraid you can't come with me for the next part of the transaction,' said Harry, 'for then you might get involved.'

'What are you going to do?'

'Just do a bit of shop-lifting,' said Harry. 'I'd never have done such a thing in the normal way. Shouldn't dream of it. But it's such a simple way out. I'll do it on a wholesale scale.

Small things, you know, but they'll add up to something under five pounds. When they see my record, they'll imagine that I've been doing it all over the place, and they'll send me for sentence. I must get at least a year – possibly two. It doesn't really matter what they give me, so long as it's enough. I can always come out whenever I want by writing to Mr Broadwas.'

'Suppose he was killed in an accident?'

'Good gracious,' said Harry, 'you're quite right. He must make an affidavit about it. We must go back there. Thank heaven you thought of it. You shall have an extra special lunch as a prize.'

They went back to Mr Broadwas and explained why they had come. He at once saw the point and agreed to make an affidavit, exhibiting the registered receipt to it, and mentioning the number of the note. This cost Harry an extra guinea, which he thought well worth while.

'Why did you mention about the Zoo?' asked Sonia.

'Just to impress myself on his memory,' replied Harry.

13 *The Shoplifter*

There are a few, a very few, genuine kleptomaniacs in the world; people who genuinely cannot help stealing when they see something to steal. These unfortunate persons do not steal consciously for greed, but because they have an irresistible impulse to do so. But for one person who really suffers from this disease – and it is a disease – there are a hundred who do not suffer from it, but, when caught stealing, pretend that they do. 'I don't know what made me do it,' the average amateur thief exclaims when caught. Of course she knows what made her do it (because these thieves are usually women). It was pure greed – purely the desire to get something for nothing, and the pleasure which the fulfilment of that desire gives.

There are also a few people, a very few people, who take something genuinely by accident and, when confronted with this fact, lose their heads and tell lies. This puts the store detective concerned into great difficulty. Is the person telling lies because she's a thief, or because she's frightened? It is sometimes impossible to tell. But there are not many of these people, any more than there are many kleptomaniacs. It is natural that real thieves should try and rely upon the defence, first of accident, and as a last resort, of illness, to try and excuse themselves.

Although the amount stolen every year is fantastically large, there is no need to shed too many tears for the shopkeepers concerned. They are under no obligation to display their goods as they do, and they would not do it unless it paid them, in spite of the losses which they sustain. Undoubtedly they do tempt weaker characters, particularly those women who have to keep their homes on a small budget. It is obvious that the amount which the stores save by employing less sales people, and the extra sales which they make by displaying their goods in such a tempting fashion must more than make up for what is lost by theft or paid in insurance.

The goods in the stores of the British Universal Stores Limited were all most attractively displayed, and there were so many varieties of them that there was almost no one who could not be tempted to buy, if not to steal.

'Now, you must disappear,' said Harry to Sonia as they reached the store where he had decided to commit his apparent crime. 'Off you go,' he said.

'Bring me back a parrot,' said Sonia.

Harry entered the store, which was crowded, and looked around him. He had taken with him a raincoat which he hung on his arm. This is one of the normal pieces of apparatus of the regular shoplifter. In addition to the thieves to whom reference has already been made, there are, of course, the professional shoplifters – people who band themselves together and make quite a good living out of regular thefts all over the country. They employ gangs who have various parts to play in the operation. For example, one may look out to see where the detective is. Another may deliberately act suspiciously without in fact taking anything in order to absorb the attention of the detective while another person actually removes the goods. First of all Harry walked into the toy department, where he selected a toy parrot and swiftly slipped it into his raincoat. The price was 2*s.* 11*d.* Then he walked to the provisions department where he selected a couple of tins of soup at 1*s.* 6*d.* each. He did not try to spot the detective or to see whether anyone was watching him. He simply went round making his haul. After twenty minutes he had taken goods to the value of something a little over four pounds, but definitely not as much as five pounds. He put on his raincoat and walked out of the shop. Nothing happened. He walked on about twenty yards and then looked round as though fearful to see whether he was being followed. He was not being followed. After making sure that no one was in fact going to question him, he had to make up his mind what to do. If he went back and disclosed what had happened, he might very well not be prosecuted. Although mistakes are sometimes made, and the foolish behaviour of some shoppers leads to their being prosecuted when in fact they have committed no offence, for the most part shops do not like prosecuting and, if the story told by the suspect is a reasonable one, in the normal way there will be no prosecution. Harry counted up exactly the price of what he had taken, and it came to four pounds, nine shillings and sevenpence. He decided to go back and take another ten shillings' worth. He also decided that he must act more suspiciously and even more obviously. He went round the shop picking up goods, looking round to see if he was observed, almost putting them in his coat pocket and then putting them down again. After he had done this two or three times, he put an article in his pocket. Then he went through the pantomime again. Then he took another article, and so on. He spent a full half-hour trying to attract suspicion to himself and taking articles to the value of 9*s.* 11*d.* Then he went out of the shop in as fearful and suspicious manner as he could and waited for something to happen. Once again, nothing happened. He walked away and still nothing happened. Now he had expended the whole of his five pounds. It is quite true that, as he had not been found out, he could probably ignore with safety the goods which he had so far taken, but, if you want to be sure that you have a cast-iron defence to a charge, you must not take any chances, however small.

Accordingly, he had to go through the same rigmarole with another firm of solicitors. This time he said it was his niece who had gone on a shoplifting spree. Mr Cantercal of Bargrove & Willett was perfectly prepared to do exactly as Harry asked him, just as Mr Broadwas had been. Once again Harry left behind five pounds in a registered envelope addressed to the British Universal Stores Limited and this time he paid a fee of two guineas in the first instance to include the cost of an affidavit in case Mr Cantercal should die too soon. Mr Cantercal was much impressed by Harry.

'I wish there were more people in the world like you, sir,' he said.

'You wouldn't make very much out of it,' said Harry.

'That's not the point,' said Mr Cantercal. 'You may be surprised to learn that lawyers do not look for work. So far from encouraging litigation, we try to discourage it. Fortunately, there are sufficient people who refuse to be discouraged.'

'Well, I'm glad to hear it,' said Harry, 'but while I'm appreciative of what you said about me, I don't really think I'm deserving of very much praise. It's only a trifle after all.'

'It isn't the amount,' said Mr Cantercal, 'it's the principle of the thing. There are too many people today who don't mind big institutions being robbed. You obviously do and I am therefore delighted to act for you. I shall post the letter myself today and I shall make my affidavit first thing tomorrow morning. That is to say, if you are prepared to risk my being run over between now and tomorrow morning.'

'I'd prefer you to do it tonight,' said Harry, 'if it's possible. I should be very sorry if you were to be run over or to have a coronary or anything of that sort, but on the other hand, I do want to be certain that the money can be proved to have been paid.'

'Very well,' said Mr Cantercal, 'I will arrange with a commissioner that I can make my affidavit tonight. I'm afraid I shall have to charge you an extra guinea, as the commissioner in this building will have gone, and I can't use anybody from my own firm. Might I ask,' he added, 'what you propose to say to your niece? Or am I being impertinent?'

'Not at all,' said Harry. 'I shall give her a lecture on *meum* and *tuum*. I shall tell her that ill-gotten gains never did anybody any good.'

'Good,' said Mr Cantercal, 'and I hope she'll heed your good advice.'

'I don't for a moment believe that she will,' said Harry, 'but the least I can do is to give it. I believe that people are dishonest or honest by nature, and that nothing can alter it. They sometimes learn to be more careful, but never to be more honest.'

'I fear you may be right,' said Mr Cantercal. 'And it is all the more to your credit that, feeling as you do, you nevertheless have taken these steps. It's extraordinary what a lot of shoplifting there is. Maybe it's because they so seldom send shoplifters to prison. Do you know that today in England there are only about a thousand women in prison. If they sent all women shoplifters to prison, I should imagine there'd be more like seven thousand.'

'Really,' said Harry, 'as many as that?'

'Well, I don't know the statistics,' said Mr Cantercal, 'but that's my guess.'

Harry thanked Mr Cantercal very much and left his offices. But he had to wait till the next day before he could achieve his object, as the next British Universal Store that he went to was just closing.

'Not even time to steal anything?' he said playfully to the manageress, who refused to let him in.

'That's not funny,' she said.

'I'm sorry,' said Harry, 'it was meant to be.'

The next day Harry went to another store.

'I hope they'll keep a better lookout,' he said to Sonia. There he adopted the same tactics, but was even more furtive. This time he was more successful. He thought he noticed a woman following his movements, and he was right. After he had collected goods to the value of between three and four pounds, he looked round him, again furtively, and left the shop. He had gone about the length of a cricket pitch when he was stopped by a man and a woman. The woman was the one whom he had suspected of being a detective.

'Excuse me, sir,' said the woman, 'have you bought any goods at British Universal Stores just there?'

'No,' said Harry, 'I can't say that I have.'

'Would you mind our looking in your raincoat?'

'I should mind very much,' said Harry.

'I believe that you have taken goods from the store and put them in your raincoat, and not paid for them.'

'Do you get a lot of that sort of thing?' said Harry.

'It's not a joke,' said the woman.

'That's what the manageress of another of your stores said to me.'

'I'm afraid I must ask you to come back with us to the store.'

'But I want to get home,' said Harry.

'I'm very sorry,' said the woman, 'but I'm afraid I must ask you to come with us.'

'Suppose I refuse?' said Harry. 'Will you call a policeman?'

'I will if necessary, but I hope you won't make it necessary.'

'Now sir,' said the manager, 'would you mind showing us what's in your raincoat pocket?'

One by one Harry produced the articles.

'Have you paid for any of these, sir?'

'Paid whom?' asked Harry.

'Paid anyone in the store?'

'No,' said Harry. 'I must admit I haven't.'

'Did you take them from the store?'

'Isn't that for you to prove?' said Harry.

'Well, I *saw* you take them,' said the woman. 'Do you dispute it?'

'Do you mean,' said Harry, 'do I call you a liar? I shouldn't dream of saying anything so offensive.'

'Well, if you haven't bought them,' said the manager, 'how do you account for their being in your pockets?'

'I suppose someone else might have put them there,' said Harry.

'Without your knowing?' said the manager.

'It *could* be done,' said Harry.

'With all these?' said the manager. 'I grant you that someone might have slipped a tin of soup or a fountain pen into your pocket, but look what you have here. Two toothbrushes, two tins of soup, a fountain pen, a toy parrot, some razor blades, a pullover and a packet of toffee. Are you really suggesting that some one person put all these into your coat?'

'Well, it may have been more than one person,' said Harry. 'We're a kindly nation, and people might have thought I looked hungry, or poor, or something of that sort, and made contributions one by one.'

'Well, if that's your only defence,' said the manager, 'I'm afraid you'll have to tell it to the magistrate. I'm now going to summon the police and prefer a charge against you.'

'I thought you said you'd only summon me.'

'That's perfectly true,' said the woman. 'If you have letters to verify your full name and address, we will take that course, as I promised to.'

'On thinking it over,' said Harry, 'I am quite happy for you to call a policeman. In fact, I'd prefer it. I'd hate to wait for a summons, and I'm told the courts are very behindhand in their work.'

'They are indeed,' said the manager. 'You might have to wait quite a time.'

'All right,' said Harry, 'fetch the policeman. May I sit down in the meantime?'

'Certainly,' said the woman.

'You didn't say "sir",' said Harry.

'I'm sorry, sir,' said the woman, smiling.

'This business of "sir" and "mister" has really got rather out of hand, hasn't it?' said Harry. 'Just because one or two judges didn't know how to behave and called all male witnesses "mister" except the prisoner, whom they called by his bare surname, some of the newspapers have run amok. They sometimes put in a "mister" and sometimes don't. Does it depend on the amount of the sentence? "Brown received a sentence of five years, Mr Jones was sentenced to three" – or does it depend upon whether he's acquitted or not? "Brown was appealing from a sentence of ten years. Mr Jones's appeal was allowed".'

A short while later a policeman appeared. Harry gave his true name and his address as Albany. The policeman cautioned him and asked him if he wished to say anything.

'Yes,' said Harry, 'I do. All I want to say is this – I'm not guilty of stealing any of these articles. It's all an unfortunate mistake, as I can prove in due course.'

Harry then went to the police station where he was formally charged. On this occasion, he said:

'It isn't stealing, I've paid for them.'

'But you've admitted you haven't,' said the police officer.

'Do you know the Judges' Rules?' said Harry. 'I'm not liable to be questioned now, am I? At any rate, I needn't answer. My failure to answer can't be used as evidence against me.'

'Very well,' said the officer, 'that's quite all right. You needn't say another word.'

Shortly afterwards Harry was released on bail and rejoined Sonia at Albany.

14 *Mass Attack*

British Universal Stores Limited in common with other big stores had suffered heavy depredations in the previous twelve months, and, as they had about twenty or thirty cases pending at the court where Harry was to be prosecuted, they decided to try and make an example and have all the cases tried consecutively. In this way they hoped that the publicity which the press was likely to give the matter would deter prospective offenders – or some of them, anyway.

So they decided to employ leading counsel, and their choice fell upon Mr Randall Blower Q.C., who was better known for his blustering at the Old Bailey than for his subtle arguments on points of law in the Court of Appeal. The magistrate was Mr Thomas, a simple and intelligent Welshman, a man both of ability and compassion and ideal for the post which he held. He still preserved a very slight Welsh accent. Any member of the legal profession who could have spared the time would have paid quite a substantial sum to be present, if he had known that Mr Blower Q.C. was going to be faced by Mr Thomas. Mr Blower was more suited to the pages of Dickens than to present-day advocacy. A few eyebrows had been raised when the Lord Chancellor recommended him for appointment as a Queen's Counsel, but someone had to be promoted from the criminal bar, and unfortunately at that particular stage the only really suitable candidates were younger men who did not apply for that distinction. The Lord Chancellor did not decide to chance his arm and appoint two of them who had not applied, in the hope that when they found their names included in the list they would accept the distinction without demur. This had happened on one occasion by accident, but the distinguished recipient of the honour decided to call attention to the fact that he hadn't applied for it, and asked for his name to be removed from the list of new silks. But Lord Chancellors do not do things by accident on purpose, and much as the then Lord Chancellor would have preferred to appoint Mr X or Mr Y rather than Mr Blower, he was not even tempted to do so.

Mr Blower having bludgeoned his way as a junior through juries and judges at the Old Bailey rightly considered that his most important stock-in-trade was a loud voice and a red face. He challenged juries to convict his guilty clients in much the same way as Horatio Bottomley did, but, whereas Horatio Bottomley only threatened the fall of the sword of justice from its scabbard, Mr Blower threatened them with every conceivable pang of conscience if they dared to convict.

'Members of the jury,' he had been heard to say, 'you daren't do it, you can't do it, you won't do it.'

But they did. Mr Blower, to his credit, was never in the least put out by these misfortunes, any more than he was put out when he had a wrangle with the judge, which was not infrequently.

'Mr Blower,' said one judge, 'you really mustn't say that. The evidence doesn't justify anything like it.'

'I can only say,' said Mr Blower, 'that I take a different view, and I propose to say so to the jury. If your lordship chooses to direct the jury that I am wrong, I cannot prevent you; I can only say so to the Court of Appeal in due course.'

'Don't be offensive, Mr Blower.'

'Your lordship leaves me no alternative.'

The directors of the British Universal Stores Limited told their solicitors that they wanted somebody who would make a fuss, somebody who would get as much publicity as possible. They knew that most of the accused would be convicted, but whether they were convicted or acquitted, what they wanted was headlines. They made it quite plain to their solicitors that they did not want a silver-tongued Norman Birkett. What they wanted was a bullying, yelling, polar bear of a man, who would grip the magistrate, the defendant and the witnesses in his huge clasp and crush them to his chest. The company's solicitors, who had never briefed Mr Blower before, were intelligent people and realised what their clients wanted. From his reputation, they considered that they could not improve on Mr Blower. They managed to get all the cases fixed for one day, and Mr Blower and a junior, who was an intelligent, but quiet young man called Sherlock, were briefed to attend the proceedings and prosecute in all the cases.

Before the hearing, the managing director attended Mr Blower's chambers for a consultation, and he was very pleased with what he found.

'This stealing,' said Mr Blower, 'is a positive scandal. It will not only be my duty, but a very great pleasure to prosecute in these cases, and I hope that the magistrate imposes exemplary sentences. I can assure you it will be from no lack of effort on my part if he does not do so. The amount of pilfering that goes on is positively disgraceful. I shall tell the magistrate so in no uncertain terms. Now, I have been carefully through all these cases and the offenders are obviously guilty in each case, but one or two of them may escape. I shall do my best to prevent this, but I can't guarantee success in every case.'

'Quite so,' said the managing director. 'I don't expect you to succeed in every case.'

'Thank you very much,' said Mr Blower, 'but let's hope we shall both be surprised. It wouldn't be the first time that I've won every case in which I've been briefed. In fact, I don't think it's an exaggeration to say that last Michaelmas Term I defended twenty people at the Old Bailey – no, not that, I'm sorry – I prosecuted ten people at the Old Bailey and they were all convicted.' (So were the twenty.) 'I've read the statistics,' went on Mr Blower, 'and I can assure you that I shall bring them to the magistrate's attention. They are quite deplorable. It used to be said that we were a nation of shopkeepers. Now we're half shopkeepers and half thieves, as far as I can make out.'

'I'm delighted to hear you say all this,' said the managing director. 'It's good to know that one's counsel has his heart in the job.'

'I always have my heart in the job,' said Mr Blower. 'Even when I'm defending a rascal whom I believe to be guilty. If one's heart weren't in the job, one couldn't do it.'

'Quite so,' said the managing director. 'I'm sorry.'

'No need to apologise,' said Mr Blower. 'A lot of people think as you do. "You do believe in my case?" they say, feeling that if I believe in their case, I'm likely to do it a bit better. I can assure you that isn't so. It does so happen I believe in your case, but that's a pure coincidence. Let me tell you, Mr Throng, that if I were appearing for each of these twenty defendants, I should put up as good a defence as I could, and I should certainly appear to believe in it. That's what counsel's for. And if we only took cases in which we really did believe, we'd go out of business in no time. But these cases have opened my eyes, Mr Thrower.'

'Mr Throng,' put in the solicitor.

'Please don't interrupt,' said Mr Blower. 'Of course I get names wrong. Everybody gets names wrong. If I were interrupted every time I got a name wrong, I shouldn't be able to speak at all.'

'Pay no attention to it,' said Mr Throng.

'I wasn't,' said Mr Blower. 'I get called all sorts of names. And I don't mind. I've even been called Bloater, and Bloggs – and by a judge. I rather think he did it on purpose in order to pretend that he didn't know who I was. Now I propose we go through each one of these cases and see if there are any queries.'

One by one they went through the cases until they came to that of Harry Woodstock.

'Ah,' said Mr Blower, 'this is a really bad one. I shall ask for him to be remanded to sessions for sentence. Six months would be ridiculous in his case. With his record. He's just an ordinary criminal, but he's never been had for this before.'

'Not been caught, I imagine,' said the managing director. 'They don't get caught the first time, or the second. Indeed some of them don't get caught at all. I want them to read the papers next day. I hope you'll emphasise the additional safeguards we now use, Mr Blower, and the probability that most people will be caught in the end.'

'I read my instructions,' said Mr Blower, 'and appreciated from the start that that's what you wanted. That's what you're paying me for, and that's what you're going to get.'

On the appointed day Harry Woodstock stood in the waiting room with other defendants who had surrendered to their bail. They included a very unhappy lady, Mrs Stanway. She was very tearful and Harry tried to comfort her.

'What *will* they do to us?' she moaned. 'I don't know what made me do it.'

'Are you sure you did do it?' said Harry.

The woman stopped crying.

'What did you say?' she said.

Harry repeated: 'Are you sure you did do it?'

'What do you mean?' she said.

'What have they charged you with taking?'

'A small bottle of scent and a sponge.'

'The sort of thing you can buy anywhere?' said Harry.

'Oh, yes,' said the woman. 'All the stores have them.'

'What did you say when they stopped you?'

'I expect I said the same as I said to you. I don't know what made me do it.'

'No, you didn't,' said Harry. 'You said something rather like it. Let me think. Oh, yes. You said: "I don't know what made you think I did it".'

'How do you know I said that?' said Mrs Stanway.

'I can see it in your honest face,' said Harry. 'You wouldn't steal anything. You're not that type. It's all a horrible mistake.'

'Do you really think so?'

'Of course I do,' said Harry. 'I wouldn't say it if I didn't. Where did they find the stuff?'

'In my bag.'

'Any other things there?'

'Oh, yes, a number of things that I'd paid for.'

'Groceries, and such?' said Harry.

'That's right. And some soap.'

'So you paid for everything except the eau de cologne and the sponge?'

'How did you know it was eau de cologne?' said the woman.

'I thought you told me,' said Harry.

'No, I only said "scent".'

'Well, it was just a guess,' said Harry. 'You've never been had for this before?'

'Oh, no,' said Mrs Stanway.

'Good,' said Harry. 'Look, someone else could have put the eau de cologne in, couldn't they?'

'How do you mean?'

'Somebody who'd pinched it could have slipped it into your bag if he thought he'd got too much on him.'

'I suppose he could.'

'Now if you suddenly found in your bag a bottle of scent which you'd never bought and never taken, you'd be horrified, wouldn't you?'

'Yes, of course,' said Mrs Stanway.

'Well, that's what you were – horrified. It would look so bad, wouldn't it?'

'Of course.'

'And the sponge you could have bought anywhere, couldn't you. And what would you have paid for it? Elevenpence halfpenny, or one and six, or two shillings, or what?'

'One and four, actually – no, two and four.'

'Well, that's what happened, isn't it? You bought the sponge somewhere else, but naturally they thought, when they found the scent in your bag, that you'd taken the sponge too. The scent somebody else must have slipped into your bag. And that's all there is to it. Now, if you're lucky, nobody will say they saw you take the sponge. If they do, you'll be for the high jump, but if they don't, there's your story. Somebody else put in the scent, and you bought the sponge at another shop. Now you say all that, and see what happens.'

'But I was going to plead guilty,' said Mrs Stanway.

'That's because you're frightened,' said Harry. 'Courts are frightening places. So are policemen. It's enough to make anybody plead guilty to be charged with an offence.'

'Do you really think it will be all right?' said Mrs Stanway.

'Well, I can't guarantee it,' said Harry, 'but have a try. It can't do any harm.'

'It's the papers I'm afraid of,' said Mrs Stanway.

'That's it,' said Harry. 'It's bound to be reported in the local papers, anyway. All the press is here today and they're making a splash about it. So, if you've got to be in the papers, you might as well be acquitted as convicted, mightn't you, now?'

'Do you really think there's a chance that the magistrate will let me off?'

'Of course there is,' said Harry. 'I wouldn't lead you up the garden path.'

'Are you defending yourself too?' said Mrs Stanway.

'Yes,' said Harry. 'Certainly.'

'Are you pleading guilty?'

'Certainly not,' said Harry. 'I've paid for the goods. Why should I?'

'You've paid for them?' said the woman.

'Certainly,' said Harry. 'That's what happens in these places. It's disgraceful. They prosecute all sorts of innocent people. Like you, Mrs Stanway.'

'How did you know my name?'

'Oh, I saw it on the list and guessed,' said Harry.

'Well, I really don't know what to do,' said Mrs Stanway.

'I've told you,' said Harry. 'If you plead guilty, you'll not only have your name in the paper as being a convicted thief, but you'll have admitted it. After all, if you plead not guilty, you can always say the magistrate was wrong.'

'I hadn't thought of that,' said Mrs Stanway.

'Oh, it's very important,' said Harry.

'Elizabeth Stanway,' called a police officer.

'Good luck,' said Harry.

Mrs Stanway's case was called first because it had been understood she was pleading guilty. As soon as the case had been called, and Mrs Stanway had been put into the dock, Mr Blower rose.

'May it please you, sir,' he said, 'I appear for the prosecution in this case with my learned friend Mr – er – ,' and he turned to his junior, 'I'm so sorry I've forgotten your name.'

'Sherlock,' said his junior.

'Mr Shertock. The defendant is not represented.'

'Just one moment, please,' said the magistrate. 'The defendant has not yet pleaded.'

'I thought you would like to know the names of counsel for the prosecution,' said Mr Blower, who was not going to be sat upon by a mere magistrate.

'I knew them already,' said Mr Thomas. 'Read out the charge, please.'

Mrs Stanway was asked if she wanted to be tried before the magistrate or before a jury and she said: 'Before the magistrate'. She was then asked how she pleaded.

'Do you plead guilty or not guilty?'

Mrs Stanway hesitated, and then in a voice that could hardly be heard, eventually said:

'Not guilty.'

'Did she say "not guilty"?' said Mr Blower.

'Yes,' said the clerk.

'That's contrary to my instructions,' said Mr Blower.

'That's a most improper observation,' said the magistrate.

'It was nothing of the kind,' said Mr Blower. 'And I tell you, sir, I'm not going to be spoken to like that.'

'If you do not wish to appear before me,' said Mr Thomas, 'there is no need for you to do so. Every time you make an improper observation I shall say so if I think fit. Now let's get on with the case. We have rather a large number of cases today.'

'That is a matter to which I wish to draw your attention, sir,' said Mr Blower. 'I am prosecuting in all these twenty cases, which are brought by the British Universal Stores Limited, and I want to tell your worship at once—', but the magistrate interrupted.

'Mr Blower,' he said, 'you may want to tell me a lot of things at once, but you are not to say anything about any case, except the one which is now in front of me. As far as *that* case is concerned, the defendant having pleaded not guilty to the charge, you will kindly open the facts to me as shortly as possible.'

'May it please you, sir,' said Mr Blower, who was advocate enough to know that if you cannot climb over the wall, you may be able to go round it, 'this is a typical case of shoplifting, typical of all the cases that you are going to hear later in the day, typical, I may say, of the cases which result in millions of pounds' worth of goods being stolen all over the country.'

'Mr Blower,' said the magistrate, 'I am only concerned in this case whether the defendant stole a bottle of scent and a sponge. Kindly confine your opening to those matters.'

'If your honour thinks you are going to teach me how to open a case,' said Mr Blower, 'I'm afraid you're very much mistaken. I shall open the case as I think fit, not as you tell me to.'

'Well, it may save time,' said the magistrate, 'if I tell you here and now that I shall disregard anything you say which is not relevant to this *one* case I am now trying, which concerns property to the value, I think, of seven shillings and elevenpence.'

'Multiply that by a million,' said Mr Blower, 'and you will still not reach the amount of money represented by the goods which are stolen.'

'I am not going to multiply it at all,' said the magistrate. 'Do you wish to say anything about this case before you call the evidence or not?'

'Very well, sir,' said Mr Blower, and looking at the press box rather than at the magistrate, he went on, 'this is a typical case of shoplifting. The defendant was caught red-handed and said, as many defendants do say in the circumstances, "I don't know what made me do it,"—'

'Please sir,' said Mrs Stanway, 'I didn't say that.'

'Now, Mrs Stanway,' said the magistrate, 'you'll be given every opportunity to tell me your case in due course, but please don't interrupt counsel for the moment.'

'I'm sorry, sir,' said Mrs Stanway, 'I've never been in these places before.'

'Quite so,' said the magistrate.

Eventually Mr Blower called his evidence. No one had actually seen Mrs Stanway take the articles, but her behaviour had excited suspicion and particular care was taken to see what articles she paid for. She did not pay for the scent or the sponge. After she had left the store, the detective followed her and asked her what she had in her bag. She showed him. When the detective pulled out the scent and the sponge, she said, 'I don't know what made me do it.' When the detective had given her evidence Mrs Stanway was asked if she would like to question the witness.

'I don't know how to,' said Mrs Stanway.

'Well,' said the magistrate, 'if you don't agree with anything which the detective has said, you tell me and I'll ask the question.'

'Well, most of what she said was right,' said Mrs Stanway.

'Well, what was wrong?'

'I didn't say: "I don't know what made me do it". I said: "I don't know what made you think I did it".'

'Did she say that?' asked the magistrate.

'No,' answered the witness, 'she said: "I don't know what made me do it".'

'Was she very upset?' said the magistrate.

'Yes, she seemed to be.'

'Anything else wrong in the detective's evidence?' asked the magistrate.

'I didn't take the things,' said Mrs Stanway.

'But you had them in your bag?'

'Oh, yes,' said Mrs Stanway.

'Very well, then.'

Eventually Mrs Stanway gave evidence and told the story that Harry had suggested.

'I don't know where the scent came from,' she said, 'and I was so flummoxed when I saw it in the bag, knowing that I'd never put it there, I didn't know what to say about it, and I thought they might think I'd taken it. But the sponge I'd bought somewhere else, and paid two shillings and fourpence for it.'

'Do you wish to cross-examine, Mr Blower?' asked the magistrate.

'I do indeed,' said Mr Blower, and rose ponderously. He said nothing for a moment and let Mrs Stanway have a good look at his large bulk and his red face. He had found by experience that this often had a paralysing effect on witnesses. Eventually he spoke.

'Now, madam,' he began and paused again. 'You stole these articles, didn't you?'

'No,' said Mrs Stanway, falteringly.

'Well, you didn't pay for them?'

'I paid for the sponge,' said Mrs Stanway.

'You didn't pay my clients for the sponge,' said Mr Blower.

'No,' said Mrs Stanway.

'And you didn't pay my clients for the scent, did you?'

'No,' said Mrs Stanway, 'I didn't.'

'Tell me, Mrs Stanway,' said Mr Blower, 'did you have a bath on the day in question?'

'I bath on Fridays,' said Mrs Stanway.

'Well, this was a Monday,' said Mr Blower. 'Did you have a bath that day?'

'No,' said Mrs Stanway, 'I didn't.'

'But I take it you washed?' said Mr Blower.

'Of course,' said Mrs Stanway.

'Well, how do you think the bottle of scent got in your bag?' said Mr Blower. 'Are you suggesting that someone came sniffing round you and, deciding that you didn't smell all that clean, said: "This lady could do with a bottle of scent" and put one in that bag?'

'That's an extremely offensive way of putting the question,' said the magistrate.

'It's not in the least offensive,' said Mr Blower. 'I suggest that this lady is a clean lady, and didn't need a bottle of scent to stop her from smelling. You didn't, did you?' persisted Mr Blower to the witness.

'I don't know what to say,' said Mrs Stanway. 'I'm all confused.'

'Don't worry, Mrs Stanway,' said the magistrate. 'Counsel was merely being unpleasantly sarcastic.'

'I desire to enter a strong protest,' said Mr Blower.

'You can enter as many protests as you like,' said the magistrate, 'but, if you continue to be unpleasantly sarcastic to the witness, I shall say so.'

'I hope,' said Mr Blower, 'that I shall be allowed to cross-examine the witness in my own way.'

'Well, you won't,' said the magistrate, 'unless you observe the normal rules of courtesy.'

'I'm not used to this sort of treatment,' said Mr Blower.

'Well,' said the magistrate, with a slight smile, 'I gather you're in all the next cases, so by the end of the day I hope you will be.'

'If necessary,' said Mr Blower, 'I shall ask for these cases to be transferred to a different magistrate.'

'I shall deal with such an application when you make it,' said the magistrate.

'Well, I make it now,' said Mr Blower.

'It is refused,' said the magistrate.

'You haven't heard the grounds yet.'

'I'm sorry,' said the magistrate, 'I thought the grounds were that I had reproved you for being unnecessarily offensive to the witness, and told you that I should go on doing so. And that in those circumstances you preferred these cases to be tried before another magistrate. If you have any other grounds for wanting a transfer, kindly state them.'

'My grounds are,' said Mr Blower, 'that you've already made up your mind in advance that you will obstruct in every way possible counsel for the prosecution.' He paused. The magistrate said nothing. Mr Blower repeated the statement.

'Anything else?' asked the magistrate.

'I should have thought that was sufficient,' said Mr Blower. 'Justice in this country has not only to be done, but to be manifestly seen to be done.'

'Do you wish to add anything to your submission?'

'There doesn't seem any point,' said Mr Blower, 'if you've made up your mind already.'

'Mr Blower,' said the magistrate, 'I'm afraid that, if you continue to address me in this way, I shall have no alternative but to report you to the Benchers of your Inn.'

'I've already made up my mind,' said Mr Blower, 'to report you to the Lord Chancellor.'

'Let us take it,' said the magistrate quietly, 'that both reports will be made. And now please, shall we get on with the case? If you have nothing else to add to your application for a transfer of this case, your application is refused.'

'Very well, sir,' said Mr Blower. 'Now may I go on cross-examining the witness?'

'By all means,' said the magistrate, 'provided you do so properly.'

'Mrs Stanway, perhaps you'll answer this question, unless the learned magistrate thinks it's improper. Why do you think anyone else should put a bottle of scent into your bag?'

'Perhaps he'd taken too many.'

'Perhaps who'd taken too many?'

'The person who took them.'

'I don't understand,' said Mr Blower. 'Why should he give you one?'

'In case he was found out.'

'You mean,' said the magistrate, 'that you suggest that some-one else may have taken this bottle of scent and others as well, and, being frightened that he was suspected, unloaded some of them, and one of them on you?'

'If you're going to answer the questions, sir,' said Mr Blower, 'perhaps I can cross-examine you instead of the witness.' The magistrate ignored Mr Blower and asked the witness:

'Is that what you mean?'

'Yes, sir,' said Mrs Stanway.

'So some kindly person off-loaded the scent on you, Mrs Stanway. What about the sponge?' asked Mr Blower. 'Was that to wipe off the scent?'

'I bought that,' said Mrs Stanway.

'Where from?' said Mr Blower.

'From Warwick and Grainger.'

'When had you bought it?'

'The same morning.'

'Did you buy anything else there?'

'No.'

'Why did you only buy a sponge there and buy all these other things at British Universal Stores?'

'Perhaps your clients sell them cheaper,' said the magistrate.

'I give up,' said Mr Blower and sat down.

'I should like to see the manager back in the witness-box, please,' said the magistrate. 'Tell me,' he went on, when the witness had returned to the box, 'were there more bottles of scent stolen than were found on Mrs Stanway?'

'That is so,' said the witness.

'And what about sponges? Was there more than one sponge stolen?'

'Yes,' said the manager.

'So that whether or not Mrs Stanway is a thief, there was more than one thief in the store that day?'

'We've always got more than one, I'm afraid,' said the manager.

'Any question you would like to ask, Mr Blower?'

Mr Blower shook his head.

'Thank you,' said the magistrate. 'There's a doubt in this case,' he went on. 'You're discharged,' he said to Mrs Stanway. The astonished Mrs Stanway went out of court as fast as she could and looked for Harry. When she found him she put her arms round his neck and hugged him.

'Oh, thank you, thank you,' she said.

'Don't mention it,' said Harry. 'Always pleased to oblige.'

'Can I come to you next time?' said Mrs Stanway.

'If you're sensible,' said Harry, 'there won't be a next time, and if there is, you won't find me here to advise you. Take my word for it. It doesn't pay.'

'Then why did you do it?' asked Mrs Stanway.

'I didn't,' said Harry. 'I told you. It was a mistake. Like yours – a different mistake – but I pay for what I buy. You do the same.'

'I think I will,' said Mrs Stanway. 'You're a good man. I'm glad I met you.'

There were so many cases that Harry's did not come on till the next day. By this time twelve had pleaded guilty, four had been convicted, and two acquitted. On the whole Mr Blower was not dissatisfied with the results, although he regarded the acquittal of Mrs Stanway as an enormity, as indeed it was, though the magistrate could hardly be blamed for the view which he took of it.

When Harry's case was called on he elected to be tried by the magistrate and pleaded Not Guilty. Mr Blower rose again.

'I'm going to spend a little more time on opening this case,' he said to the magistrate, who repressed a sigh. 'My clients take a very serious view of it, as I suggest you should. In the view of the prosecution this accused is not a normal shoplifter, and by that I'm not simply referring to the amateur type of shoplifter, but he's not an ordinary professional shoplifter either. He is simply a criminal stealing. He's an educated man who prefers that method of earning his living to an honest one.'

At that moment the magistrate intervened.

'Forgive me, Mr Blower,' he said. 'Mr Woodstock,' he said, 'would you like this case to be reheard before another magistrate?'

'No, thank you sir,' said Harry.

'You're quite sure?' said the magistrate.

'I'm very happy with your worship,' said Harry.

'Well, I'm not sure that you ought to be,' said the magistrate. 'Now, I don't want you to answer any question or say anything except whether you've changed your mind and would like to be tried by someone else. What counsel for the prosecution has tried to do, and in my view he's done it very successfully, is to indicate to me that you've had previous convictions for crime, which everyone in the legal world knows perfectly well should not be mentioned to a magistrate or a jury when they are trying a person for a crime.'

'I said nothing of the kind,' said Mr Blower.

'You said,' said the magistrate, 'that Mr Woodstock prefers to live by crime rather than earn an honest living. The goods he is alleged to have stolen in this case amount in value to something under five pounds. How do you expect him to live on that?'

'If he does it often enough,' said Mr Blower cheerfully, 'he could make a very fat living. Three times in the morning, three times in the afternoon, only five days a week, would do very nicely. What I am suggesting in this case is that the way in which the crime was committed showed that the accused was a regular perpetrator of such crimes.'

'Well,' said the magistrate, 'as I mentioned the matter, I had better grasp the nettle and go into it fully. Are you suggesting that he's got previous convictions for shoplifting?'

'No,' said Mr Blower, 'not for shoplifting.'

'Mr Blower,' said the magistrate, 'you have shown by many of the things you've said this morning and this afternoon that your sense of responsibility as a member of the Bar is not all that could be desired. But, unless you were trying to convey to me that the defendant has previous convictions, I cannot think why you added the words "not for shoplifting", or why you emphasised them in the way that you did.'

'Because,' said Mr Blower, 'it happens to be the truth. The defendant has no convictions for shoplifting. That is so, Mr Woodstock, is it not?'

'It is,' said Harry.

'If I may say so, sir,' said Mr Blower, 'what you seem to object to is my stating facts which are agreed on both sides.'

'Well, Mr Woodstock,' said the magistrate, 'have you followed what's been going on?'

'Perfectly,' said Harry. 'I would like your worship to go on trying the case. And may I add something?'

'What is it?' said the magistrate.

'I would like Mr Blower to go on prosecuting,' said Harry.

'Well, at any rate,' said Mr Blower, 'I'm glad the defendant thinks I'm fair.'

The magistrate's eyes met Harry's, but neither of them spoke. The magistrate thought for about half a minute and then said:

'You're obviously an intelligent man, Mr Woodstock, and, if you want me to go on trying the case in order to avoid an adjournment, I will do so. It will save money and trouble all round, and I hope I am capable of disregarding the implied suggestions which have been made against your character. Do you wish to add anything before calling your evidence, Mr Blower?'

'I do indeed,' said Mr Blower. 'The accused has pleaded Not Guilty and it is right that you should know first from me what the prosecution say he has done, so that you can compare my opening with the evidence of the witnesses, and decide whether they bear it out. I repeat that this is a very serious case and I should like to warn the public, particularly the criminal and semi-criminal elements in it, that my clients, British Universal Stores Limited, have very special methods of detecting this sort of crime and that the chances of their being able to steal goods from our stores undetected are very small indeed. If they want to steal, they will not find it a good bet to try and steal from British Universal Stores.'

'Are you suggesting,' said the magistrate, 'that they should turn their attention to, say, Messrs Warwick and Grainger?'

'And now, sir,' said Mr Blower, 'I suppose you're accusing me of incitement to felony. Of course I meant no such thing. I hope that eventually all stores will use the methods adopted by my clients, and when they do this form of crime will pretty well be stamped out. I want to emphasise that fact very strongly indeed, and I hope that the gentlemen of the Press, who normally discharge their duties to the public so well, will particularly take note.'

'Are you addressing me, or the newspapers?' asked the magistrate.

'This is a public hearing,' said Mr Blower, 'and it is right that the public should know what is happening. There is only room for about thirty or forty members of the public in court, and, if it weren't for the members of the Press, no one would know what is happening. My clients desire, and I as a responsible member of the Bar also desire, that the facts of these cases should be publicised as much as possible. It's in the interests of the country as a whole that they should be.'

'So far, Mr Blower,' said the magistrate, 'you have not mentioned one single fact to suggest that the defendant did anything which justified your clients in putting him in the dock. You have merely alleged vaguely that he makes his living by crime. If you want to open the facts, pray do so. But, unless you are going to open the facts, I must insist on your calling the evidence and stopping talking.'

'No judge or magistrate has ever spoken to me like that before,' said Mr Blower.

'From that,' said the magistrate, 'I must assume that this is the first time that you have behaved in this extraordinary way.'

'I have been a member of the Bar for twenty years,' said Mr Blower. 'I have appeared before every type of judge and magistrate, from the House of Lords down to you, and no one has yet treated me with the scant courtesy shown to me by you.'

'What about the facts?' asked the magistrate.

'I shall come to those,' said Mr Blower, 'in my own good time.'

'I'm afraid not,' said the magistrate, 'you'll come to them now, or not at all.'

'Indeed, sir?' said Mr Blower. 'My clients, British Universal Stores Limited—'

'Call your evidence, please,' interrupted the magistrate.

'You didn't know what I was going to say,' said Mr Blower.

'I've given you ample opportunity to open the facts,' said the magistrate, 'and, as you apparently are not prepared to do so, without putting in a lot of matter which to my mind is entirely irrelevant, at any rate at this stage of the case, I'm not going to have my time, or the court's time, or the accused's time, or the other witnesses' time wasted any longer. Please call your evidence.'

'Are you telling me, sir,' said Mr Blower, 'that you will not listen to me any longer? Do I rightly understand that?'

'Perfectly,' said the magistrate.

'I can only say,' said Mr Blower, 'that I shall go to the Divisional Court to get an order commanding you to listen to me.'

'Do you apply for an adjournment in order that you may do so?' asked the magistrate.

'I will take instructions,' said Mr Blower, and he spoke to his solicitor who was sitting in front of him.

'I think we've got it all in,' he whispered, 'shall we leave it at that?' The solicitor nodded.

'I've spoken to my clients,' said Mr Blower to the magistrate. 'They do not want the additional expense or delay involved. In those circumstances, under protest, I will defer to your ruling and call my evidence.'

The first witness was the manager of the store who gave evidence that the goods taken by Harry were in fact missing from the store. Harry was invited to cross-examine.

'But they weren't the only goods taken that morning, were they?' he asked.

'No,' said the manager.

'My little lot came to four pounds, eleven, I think?'

'Yes,' said the manager.

'What was the total for that morning?'

'I object,' said Mr Blower.

'On what grounds?' asked the magistrate.

'On the grounds that the question is totally irrelevant.'

'I don't know,' said the magistrate, 'it may be relevant, it may not be. I don't know what the defence is yet. I don't see how it can do your clients any harm to answer. I suppose you'd say that it might possibly show that the precautions to which you referred a little while ago were not as adequate as they might be.'

'You've no right to say that,' said Mr Blower.

'Well,' said the magistrate, 'I shall allow the question, but if you would prefer the answer to be written down, I don't see that that will hurt anybody. Would you prefer to write it down?' he asked the manager.

'Yes, please.'

So a piece of paper was brought and the manager wrote down '£50 3*s.* 4*d.*' on it. The paper was handed to the magistrate who ordered that it should be shown to Harry, and then destroyed.

'Was that a particularly bad day?' asked Harry.

'It wasn't a good day,' said the manager.

'Did you catch anyone besides me?'

'Yes,' said the manager, 'we caught three others.'

'Have they been tried yet?'

'Yes,' said the manager.

'And what happened?'

'They pleaded guilty.'

'That's all I wish to ask,' said Harry.

Mr Blower then called the store detective who described

Harry's suspicious movements and how she had personally seen him take the goods mentioned in the charges.

'Tell me,' said Harry, when he had been invited to cross-examine, 'did I take them in an open way in which you'd expect a person who was going to pay for the goods to take them, or did I take them in a furtive way?'

'Well, you asked the question,' said the detective, 'do you want me to answer it?'

'Yes,' said Harry, 'that's why I asked it.'

'Are you sure?' said the detective.

'Certainly,' said Harry. 'You're on oath and I'm sure you wouldn't tell a lie.'

'No, I wouldn't,' said the detective, 'and, as I won't tell a lie, the truth is that you took them in an extremely furtive manner.'

'Would you say,' said Harry, 'that I took them almost in a manner that suggested I wanted to be caught?'

The detective thought for a moment.

'Yes,' she said, 'I think that's a very fair way of putting it.'

'And will you repeat what I said when you stopped me and asked me about the goods.'

'You said you hadn't stolen them,' said the detective.

'Did I seem worried, or upset in any way?'

'No,' said the detective, 'I can't say you did.'

'And did I answer your questions quite openly, and without hesitation?'

'I think so,' said the detective.

'Did I admit taking the goods?'

'You did.'

'Did you ask me whether I'd paid anybody in the store?'

'I did.'

'And what did I say?'

'You said you hadn't.'

'So you had what you thought was an open and shut case?' said Harry. 'A man seen taking the goods furtively, walking out of the shop, admitting that he'd taken them, and that he'd not paid?'

'That's right,' said the detective.

'But,' said Harry, 'I did say I hadn't stolen them, didn't I?'

'You did.'

'And did you ask me if I was going to pay for them?'

'I did.'

'And did I say that I wasn't?'

'You did.'

'I didn't try to avoid arrest, or run away, or anything like that?' asked Harry.

'No, you didn't.'

'You say that I was furtive in the way that I took the goods. Was there anything furtive in the way I answered your questions or behaved when you challenged me?'

'No,' said the detective, 'I can't say that there was.'

'That's all that I wish to ask, sir,' said Harry.

'That is the case, sir,' said Mr Blower.

Harry was then asked if he would like to go in the witness-box, or whether he wanted to make a statement from where he was. He said that he would like to make a statement from the dock. Mr Blower rose; he would have liked the opportunity to cross-examine Harry. Although the case on the face of it was completely proved, he would have enjoyed dragging it out of the defendant once or twice more. But, if Harry only made a statement from the dock, he could not ask him any questions at all.

'I hope, sir,' he said, 'that the defendant realises that, if he only makes a statement from the dock and cannot be cross-examined, it will not carry as much weight as though he had given evidence.'

'You do realise that, do you?' asked the magistrate of Harry.

'Yes, your worship, I do.'

'Well,' said Mr Blower, 'if you have got a defence to the case, it seems a pity that you don't go in the witness-box and say what it is.'

'You have no right to speak to the accused like that,' said the magistrate. 'You shouldn't speak to him at all.'

'Someone ought to point out to him his legal rights,' said Mr Blower. 'I've had a good many years' experience of criminal practice, and there are quite a lot of people who do not appreciate the importance of giving evidence on oath, rather than making a statement from the dock. A statement from the dock carries no weight at all.'

'That's not correct,' said the magistrate. 'Of course it doesn't carry as much weight as a statement about which the accused can be cross-examined. But it *may* affect the mind of the person trying the case.'

'Of course,' said Mr Blower, 'some people don't like giving evidence, because they could be convicted of perjury if they did. I'm sure that isn't so in Mr Woodstock's case,' he added.

'It is, as a matter of fact,' said Harry.

'You admit, then, that you're going to tell lies to the magistrate?'

'Be quiet, Mr Blower,' said the magistrate. 'This is really quite intolerable. Mr Woodstock,' he went on, 'what do you want to say about this?'

'Just this, your worship,' said Harry. 'Everything that the witnesses have said is true but I'm not guilty.'

'Do you want to explain what appears to be a contradiction?' asked the magistrate.

'No, thank you, sir,' said Harry.

'Well, on the evidence,' said Mr Thomas, 'I find this case proved.'

'Now,' said Mr Blower, 'I can tell you what I've been careful not to tell you before. The accused has many previous convictions for crime of one sort or another.'

'But not for shoplifting,' said the magistrate.

'No,' said Mr Blower, 'not for shoplifting. That I did tell you before.'

'You did indeed,' said the magistrate.

'In the circumstances,' said Mr Blower, 'I ask you to send him to sessions for sentence. The maximum period of imprisonment which you can award is wholly insufficient for a man of his record.'

'What do you say, Mr Woodstock?' asked the magistrate.

'If I may say so,' said Harry, 'I think it's the right course to take. May I thank your worship for the very great courtesy which you have shown to me in trying the case. I should also like to thank Mr Blower for his contribution. Next time perhaps he'll be appearing for me.'

'Behave yourself, Mr Woodstock, please,' said the magistrate.

Harry was then removed from the court.

15 *A Carrot But No Donkey*

Harry eventually received a sentence of three years' imprisonment, and the disappointed Stephen, who had been unable to locate Harry in a place where he could conveniently confront him, went back to Portugal. Meanwhile, Harry returned to Albany.

It was not long before he received a visit from the canon.

'Well, here we are again,' said Harry. 'The same old story. But I was damned lucky. I heard that Stratford was back over here, and I didn't get inside any too quickly.' He explained to the canon the circumstances in which he had returned to prison on this occasion.

'Did you see Sonia while you were out?' asked the canon.

'Trust you to find a sore spot,' said Harry. 'Yes, I did. I'm really worried about her.'

'Do you think she may do something silly?' asked the canon.

'It's I who may do something silly,' said Harry. 'If I'm not careful, I may marry the girl. She says she's never met a man like me. Well, I'm glad to hear it. I've certainly never met a girl like her. Oh, I expect there are lots of nice girls like her, but we've all got slightly different wave-lengths, and unfortunately, she's exactly on mine.'

'Well,' said the canon, 'let's hope they catch Mr Stratford, and then you can marry and settle down and live happily ever after. How did you know he was over here, by the way?'

'Oh,' said Harry, 'I heard things.'

'How?'

'That would be telling,' said Harry. 'I devoutly hope that they'll catch him, but I'd never be happy if I had any part in it. Isn't it odd?'

'Not in the least odd,' said the canon. 'You have far more principles than several businessmen I know, who've never committed a crime in their lives. You're a good man.'

'That's the second time I've been told that,' said Harry.

'When was the first?'

'A shoplifter I'd helped told me. I told her a good story to tell. She told it and got off, so she said I was a good man. Well, I was from her point of view.'

'You mean,' said the canon, 'that you incited her to commit perjury?'

'Well, that's a harsh way of putting it,' said Harry, 'but no doubt it's right.'

'Why on earth did you do a thing like that?'

'I was sorry for the woman.'

'What about the people she stole from?'

'British Universal Stores Limited,' said Harry. 'Now don't ask me to be sorry for them.'

'They're made up of people,' said the canon.

'The assistants wouldn't get into trouble for what I did,' said Harry, 'and as for the directors and all those people, they seem to be able to look after themselves all right. You can't expect me to be sorry for people who have car numbers with their initials and "1" after them.'

'They may be very unhappy men,' said the canon.

'Oh,' said Harry, 'I could be sorry for anyone in particular. He might have a dreadful wife, or a criminal son, or something of that sort. He might have an accident and be paralysed for life. I'd be very sorry for him then. But I can't be sorry for such people as British Universal Stores in general, and I can be sorry for a silly little woman who steals from them.'

'I think you could have got five years for what you did,' said the canon.

'No doubt,' said Harry. 'It won't be the first crime I've committed and got nothing for. But if it's the worst thing I've ever done, I shall sleep easy at nights. I sleep well anyway. The only person who's kept me awake is Sonia.'

'Well, I'm glad to hear that,' said the canon. 'Where will you live when you get married?'

'Wherever she likes,' said Harry. 'Now what have you made me say? There's a conspiracy, and you're in it.'

'Well,' said the canon, 'I hope there is. And if there is one, God and I are in it.'

'A nice partner to have,' said Harry. 'He'd be useful in my business.'

'You can have him,' said the canon.

'Can I put him on the notepaper?' said Harry. 'Harry Woodstock, God and Partners – no, I suppose it ought to be the other way round – God, Woodstock and Partners. It would look rather nice, wouldn't it?'

'God will be a partner to anyone who wants him,' said the canon.

'Will he take on the chairmanship of a limited company? That would look well, too. "Chairman and Managing Director – God".'

'He's Chairman and Managing Director of the whole world,' said the canon.

'Does he hold all the shares?' asked Harry.

'He's ready to hold any share that anyone wants him to hold.'

'Who are the co-directors?' asked Harry.

'You and I and everyone else who wants to be,' said the canon.

'Well, if he runs the whole world, why doesn't he tell Russia to lay off Czechoslovakia, or things like that?'

'Because he doesn't run it that way,' said the canon. 'Man must work out his own salvation. God is with us all whenever we want him. He suffers long and is kind. He rejoices in the truth.'

'Surely, that was love,' said Harry.

'It's the same thing,' said the canon. 'You can say it anyway you like. God is Love, God is Truth, Truth is God, Love is God. The truth and love in you are God. You are part of God. He is part of you.'

'Was he with me when I pinched those things from the British Universal Stores?'

'Certainly,' said the canon.

'Did he approve?'

'Well, in your case,' said the canon, 'I don't suppose he minded very much. Even though you committed a crime.'

'What crime?' asked Harry.

'I think they call it "creating a public mischief".'

'What can I get for that?'

'I don't know. A couple of years, I suppose.'

'So even if I get this sentence quashed, they can give me a couple of years for the other?'

'You must ask a lawyer about that. But I should think so. After all, you were a confounded nuisance. You pretended to steal, and the law had to be set in motion. You caused a lot of trouble and expense. You're being kept for nothing in prison. It *ought* to be an offence, even if it isn't.'

'You mean getting myself locked up in prison is an offence for which I can be sent to prison?'

'Yes,' said the canon.

'Well, that's one way of going to prison, isn't it? So there doesn't seem much point in the end. The law says "here's a man who commits an offence by getting sent to prison, so we'll send him to prison". That's what he wants, so what's the law getting out of it?'

'Well, you'd better say that in mitigation of sentence,' said the canon, 'when the time comes. But I confess, I hope it won't.'

'You'd like to see Stratford in prison and me out, wouldn't you?' asked Harry.

'Yes,' said the canon, 'I certainly would.'

'Well, what do you know about him? Why are you so down on him? He may be a much better man than me.'

'He's a would-be murderer,' said the canon. 'Those bank clerks and those other people might have been killed, and he wouldn't have cared. You're not like that.'

'I don't use firearms, I grant you,' said Harry. 'Otherwise people might use them back on me. But I've cheated people out of their money for years. I prefer to do it my way. He prefers to do it his.'

'Your way,' said the canon, 'doesn't hurt or maim people.'

'It makes them damned angry,' said Harry. 'They might get in a temper and kill somebody.'

'That's too far-fetched,' said the canon.

'Tell me,' said Harry, 'if – only *if*, mind you – if I married Sonia, would you marry us?'

'I can't think of anything I'd like better,' said the canon.

'How about being Archbishop of Canterbury – would you like that better?' asked Harry.

'No, I wouldn't,' said the canon, 'I wouldn't like the responsibility.'

'Or York?' said Harry.

'No,' said the canon. 'From my point of view that'd be the same thing.'

'You shirk responsibility, then?' asked Harry.

'Yes, you could say that,' said the canon. 'But perhaps that isn't fair to myself. I like dealing with small things, not the larger. I like dealing with the less important people, not the more important.'

'I thought everyone was important to God,' said Harry. 'Am I more important, then, to God than a director of British Universal Stores?'

'No,' said the canon, 'you're quite right. He makes no distinctions.'

'You seem to know a lot about him,' said Harry. 'Has he let you into his confidence?'

'Yes,' said the canon, 'I think he has.'

'Where did you first meet him?' asked Harry.

'That's a good question,' said the canon. 'It's difficult to say, but I'm glad to say that it was a long time ago.'

'Is he a vegetarian?' asked Harry.

'You mean,' said the canon, 'why does he create animals to be killed? If he's all-loving and all-powerful, why does he do that? And still worse, why does he create animals to prey on each other, to torture each other before they make their kill? You ask me to explain why God made the spider and the fly, the cat and the mouse, and so on.'

'I didn't,' said Harry, 'but I'd like to hear you.'

'Well,' said the canon, 'a lot of people do try to explain. Some people are even reduced to saying that we can't be sure that animals really feel pain in the way we understand it. In my view, people who say that are guilty of intellectual dishonesty. If you stand on a dog's tail, it yelps – it yelps because it hurts, and if the pain-waves or whatever you call them, aren't *exactly* the same as I should feel if you stamped on my toe, or as I did when you punched my jaw, all the indications are that there's not much difference between them. Of course, you can say that the fly doesn't feel anything when the spider stings it to death, that fishes are cold-blooded and don't feel anything, and the same with other insects. But you can't say that about the stoat and the rabbit, or the greyhound and the hare.'

'Well,' said Harry, 'you're saying all these things. Now tell me the answer. Here's your all-loving, all-powerful God who lets me go to prison because it's good for me, who lets litlet children be burned or scalded or run over because man has got to work out his own salvation, letting the spider and the fly work out their own salvation. Have animals, insects and microbes got souls to be saved? It's very difficult for me to think that the virus which gives me a cold has a soul. It's very difficult to think that a spider has a soul any more than a virus or germ or microbe. If it hasn't, why does God permit such cruelty in the animal and the insect world?'

'Those are all very fair questions,' said the canon. 'In my view there is only one truthful answer that can be given. And that is that I don't know, but I still believe.'

'What do you tell children when they ask these questions?'

'The same as I've told you,' said the canon. 'I cannot profess to understand the working of God's mind in the creation of the world and everything in it. I can only say that wherever there is truth, wherever there is love, there is God.'

'Well, you don't find much love in the things I've been talking about,' said Harry; 'the spider and the fly, the cat and the mouse.'

'No,' said the canon, 'I agree, there isn't. Not that we can see. They're horrible things, and I cannot explain them. There are many things in the world that are beyond our comprehension. We should be supermen if there were not.'

'You admit, then,' said Harry, 'that there's a pretty strong case against God for cruelty to animals? I'd like to hear Mr Blower open it.'

'I admit only that I cannot explain these things,' said the canon. 'Now, I've done my best to answer your questions. Will you answer one of mine? If Stratford's caught and you come out and marry Sonia, you'll be going straight, I suppose?'

'I'm afraid so,' said Harry. 'It goes against the grain, but I don't see any alternative.'

'Well, how will you make your living?' asked the canon.

'You may well ask that,' said Harry. 'It won't be any too easy. But, if I'm going to make an honest living, I can't give false references. That's rather fun, by the way. The great thing is not to overdo it. Then people get suspicious. But if you simply say that "the Global Confectionery Company has been trading with us for the last six months, and although the account has been a small one, we've had no reason to complain about lack of proper payment", that has a genuine ring about it. Or how about this? "We have done substantial business with the Global Confectionery Company Ltd over the last two years, and the account at the moment is clear, but it is only right to say that about six months ago they owed us a considerable sum, and we had to threaten the issue of proceedings before it was paid. It was, however, paid and there has been no trouble in collecting the monthly account since then." That couldn't be a false reference, could it? But the stupid references I have seen – something like, "We have traded with the Global Confectionery Company for the past twelve years. The account is an extremely large one and I am happy to say that it is always paid on the due date or sometimes even before." That sort of thing asks for trouble. I never tried it myself. It's like a reference about an employee which says he's "very honest". I remember one personal reference given to a chap which, having lauded him to the skies and said how very honest and wonderful he was, added: "Knowing him as I do, I cannot well say less." That reference, I may say, was given by a gentleman who described himself as the Baron de Pitchford. Perhaps I had better give you as a referee. "I visited Mr Harry Woodstock regularly during his prison sentences, and over the years I took a considerable liking to him. He was mainly charged with fraud. Personally, I would trust him anywhere. P.S. I have never actually been certified."'

'Seriously,' said the canon, 'if you took a job on, I would most willingly give you a reference. But, of course, I would have to explain all the circumstances. But then, it's no good your taking on a job without explaining them yourself.'

'I'm a bit old to go into a bank,' said Harry.

'Well, I bet you could get a good job,' said the canon.

'That's an idea,' said Harry, 'how about the turf? A bookie's runner, or something. I'll tell you something,' he added, 'they wouldn't have me there. They're more particular about honesty on the turf than they are anywhere else. They have to be, you see. Bets aren't enforceable, and, unless you can take a chap's word, you can't do business at all. It's amazing how honest they all are. They're a lot of thugs, of course, by nature.'

At that stage their interview was interrupted when a prison officer came along to say that a detective-inspector wanted to see Harry.

'I wonder what that will be about,' said Harry. 'Fortunately, I have a clear conscience, or as clear a conscience as usual.'

The canon left and Harry was taken to see Detective-Inspector Snowshill.

'How are you, Woodstock?' he began. 'I don't think we've met before.'

'I've heard of you, Inspector,' said Harry, 'but I don't think we've met. What can I do for you?'

'I'd just like a chat.'

'Well, it makes a change,' said Harry. 'Fire ahead.'

'Have you ever heard of a man called Stephen Stratford?'

'Of course,' said Harry. 'Everyone has.'

'Have you met him?'

'Not to my knowledge. Have you?'

'I'm asking the questions,' said the inspector.

'Sorry,' said Harry. 'I was just trying to keep the conversation going.'

'It isn't flagging yet,' said the inspector.

'I'll be sorry when it does,' said Harry.

'Have you ever had anything to do with Stephen Stratford?'

'Anything to do with him?' said Harry. 'Certainly not.'

'Are you sure about that?'

''Course I'm sure, unless it was something casual and I've forgotten all about it, and I didn't know who the man was. I mean, I've taken a ticket in a booking office and the man who gave me the ticket may have been called Stephen Stratford, for all I know.'

'Did you meet him in prison?' asked the inspector.

'That's possible,' said Harry. 'We meet a lot of people here.'

'Did you talk to him?'

'That's also possible.'

'Did you know who he was when you talked to him?'

'It's possible I did at the time, but if he wasn't well-known then, his name wouldn't have meant anything to me and I should have forgotten it.'

'He robbed a bank of sixty thousand pounds.'

'So I read. He got twenty years for it.'

'Thirty,' said the inspector.

'What's ten among so many?' said Harry.

'And then he escaped.'

'Yes, I knew that,' said Harry.

'We have reason to believe he hasn't yet got his sixty thousand pounds.'

'All that trouble for nothing?' said Harry. 'And thirty years into the bargain.'

'We think he gave it to somebody else for safe custody.'

'That was a stupid thing to do,' said Harry. 'There's only one person I'd give sixty thousand pounds to for safe custody. And that's the bank, or a safe deposit.'

'Perhaps the money's in a safe deposit now,' said the inspector.

'Very likely,' said Harry. 'But what's it got to do with me?'

'You wouldn't know which safe deposit it's in, I suppose?'

'Me, how on earth should I know?'

'Do you like it here?' asked the inspector.

'Tolerable,' said Harry. 'I've known worse.'

'How are you off for funds?'

'So-so.'

'The bank are offering a reward for information which leads to recovery of the money and—'

'No questions asked?' said Harry.

'They can't say that,' said the inspector, 'because that might be compounding a felony, but they don't have to ask any questions. If somebody handed over sixty thousand to them, I suspect they might hand him ten thousand pounds back.'

'Nearly twenty per cent,' said Harry. 'Suppose Mr Stratford handed them back, would they ask him no questions?'

'That would be different,' said the inspector, 'but he might get a bit knocked off the thirty years if he gave himself up and handed over the proceeds.'

'Twenty per cent?' queried Harry.

'I wouldn't put it past them,' said the inspector.

'Well, that's most interesting,' said Harry, 'but I still don't know how it concerns me.'

'Don't you?' said the inspector.

'I wouldn't say I didn't understand if I did, would I?' said Harry.

'Yes,' said the inspector. 'That's just what you would do.'

'You mean I'm a liar?' said Harry.

'That's right,' said the inspector.

'Then, what's the good of asking me questions?' said Harry. 'If I'm a liar, I might tell you a lie.'

'You never know when a bit of truth might intervene,' said the inspector. 'It's always worth asking.'

'Not on this occasion, I'm afraid,' said Harry. 'I've no idea of the whereabouts of Stratford or of his sixty thousand pounds, I mean of the bank's sixty thousand pounds.'

'If I told you that you'd be released tomorrow and get ten thousand pounds if you gave me true information on the subject, would that make any difference?'

'Could you really go as far as that?' said Harry.

'I didn't say I could,' said the inspector, 'but I asked you if it would make any difference.'

'A lot of people would have fallen for that, inspector,' said Harry. 'It's not fair. I don't know anything about it, but suppose I did, and I'd said: "All right, I'll tell you," you'd have then said: "Right, well I'll report what you've said to me and we'll see what happens." That's right, isn't it?'

'I'm not the Home Secretary,' said the inspector. 'I can't let people out of prison.'

'Of course you can't,' said Harry, 'but then you shouldn't say you would, or lead me to believe you would. Fortunately, as I've nothing to tell you, there's no temptation to me to do it.'

'Well, let's forget the sixty thousand pounds for the moment,' said the inspector. 'What about Stratford? Do you know where he is, or where he can be found?'

'Not the faintest,' said Harry.

'Now listen to this,' said the inspector. 'And listen carefully. I'm going to dot all the i's and cross all the t's. If you give me genuine information which leads to the capture of Stephen Stratford, I'll guarantee to you that you'll be out of this prison within a month.'

'And where would I be transferred?' said Harry.

'No,' said the inspector, 'this is on the level. You'd be free. On parole.'

'With police protection?'

'Certainly.'

'For as long as I wanted it?'

'Yes.'

'You must want him badly,' said Harry.

'We do,' said the inspector. 'There have been too many of these escapes and the public's getting worried. When the public gets worried, it worries us. The Commissioner of Police is worried; the head of the C.I.D. is worried; the Chief Superintendent is worried, and so on till it comes down to me. And I'm worried.'

'And now you're trying to worry me,' said Harry.

'That's right,' said the inspector. 'I hope I've succeeded. You've got a girl waiting for you outside. Don't you ever think of her?'

'Yes,' said Harry, 'unfortunately, I do.'

'Well, wouldn't it be nice to go off with her, with say five hundred pounds in your pocket, in a month's time? A couple of weeks in Brighton will do you a world of good.'

'I prefer the Isle of Wight,' said Harry.

'All right. Sandown, Shanklin, Ryde. Take your choice.'

'You'd guarantee me five hundred pounds and a release in a month if I give you information which will lead to the arrest of Stephen Stratford.'

'That's it.'

'And how much would you add to it if you got the sixty thousand pounds as well?'

'I told you. Ten thousand.'

'And suppose only part of it was there? The same percentage?'

'I don't see why not,' said the inspector.

'How many other people have you tried?' asked Harry.

'Hundreds,' said the inspector. 'But they don't know as much as you.'

'Well then, you *have* been wasting your time,' said Harry. 'I don't know anything at all. Don't you get bored sometimes when you come up against a brick wall?'

'I don't understand you,' said the inspector. 'You're a man who likes good living. When you're out you live soft, very soft. You can't like living hard here.'

'It makes me enjoy the soft all the more,' said Harry.

'You've got three years this time,' said the inspector. 'That means you'll be out in about eighteen months or so.'

'If I don't blot my copybook,' said Harry. 'I've done that once or twice, you know.'

'If you're implicated in keeping Stratford out of the way, or in looking after his sixty thousand pounds for him, you can be charged with another offence and go back inside again.'

'Of course,' said Harry. 'And if I murdered my mother, I'd go to prison for life, wouldn't I?'

'You're being very stupid,' said the inspector.

'I've been stupid all my life,' said Harry. 'Why should I stop now?'

'Well,' said the inspector, 'let's forget about my offer. I'm not asking you to tell me a thing. Just tell me if there is anything you *do* know, which you could tell me if you wanted to?'

'Is there anything I *do* know, which I could tell you if I

wanted to,' repeated Harry, and paused for a moment or two. 'Yes, I suppose there are lots of things,' he went on.

'Ah,' said the inspector. 'I thought as much.'

'But not about Stephen Stratford or his sixty thousand pounds,' said Harry. 'Lot's of things about *me*, I meant.'

'You mean other crimes you've committed which haven't yet come to light?' said the inspector.

'That's a leading question, if ever there was one,' said Harry. 'That's hitting the Judges' Rules for six.'

'It isn't, actually, said the inspector, 'though, I admit, I shouldn't mind doing so. No, I'm not out to get you for anything else. I'd like to help you, if you'd help us. Why don't you? That's a thing I can't make out. You're a crook if ever there was one. You'd cheat anybody out of anything if you got the chance. And yet, when a perfectly good offer's made to you, you turn it down.'

'It wouldn't have been honest to accept it,' said Harry. 'I've nothing to tell you. D'you know – something's just occurred to me. I'd have been obtaining money by false pretences. How terrible. And in prison, of all places.'

'All right,' said the inspector. 'I give up for the moment. But if you change your mind, you know where to get me. Just let them know you'd like to have an interview with me and I'll be round.'

'That's very good of you, inspector. Well, I hope you're less worried than you were. Even if only a trifle, you should be. You've eliminated me.'

'I've done nothing of the sort,' said the inspector. 'And I'll tell you something. All I knew when I came to see you was pure hearsay. I hadn't the faintest idea whether there was anything in it or whether there wasn't. But having seen you, although you won't tell me a thing, I know perfectly well that there's something you could tell me.'

'Well, how much do I get for that?' said Harry.

'Not a blooming thing,' said the inspector. 'But when I make my report, I shall say in it "Harry Woodstock knows", so someone else may come and see you.'

'Do you think the Commissioner would come himself?' said Harry.

'I doubt it,' said the inspector.

'Not even if I said I'd tell him, and only him?'

'Oh yes, I think he'd come then. Will you tell him if I send him?'

'I'd like to meet the Commissioner,' said Harry. 'I've heard so much about him. But, if I said yes, I'd make a pretty charlie out of you, because I wouldn't tell him when he did come. You'd become a sergeant again. But I wouldn't do a thing like that to you. If I said I'd tell the Commissioner or the head of the C.I.D., I'd tell him.'

'But you won't.'

'I've nothing to tell. It's as simple as that,' said Harry.

'Let me know if you change your mind,' said the inspector and left.

16 Another Carrot

Later in the day on which the inspector had visited Harry, a man spoke to him while on exercise. He was a cockney.

'What did he want?' he said.

'The usual,' said Harry. 'Information.'

'Did you give it?'

'Like hell I gave it,' said Harry.

'Well, if you know what's good for you, you won't.'

'I know what's good for me,' said Harry. 'Who told you to ask me?'

'I don't give nothing away, either,' said the man.

'Well, that's all right,' said Harry. 'We must have a chat sometime. It should be interesting with neither of us giving away anything.'

'Funny, aren't you?' said the man.

'No,' said Harry. 'I'm not particularly funny. In fact, I'm rather a bore.'

'Well, you can chase yourself for all I care,' said the man, but he didn't say 'chase'.

Later that day Harry was sent for by the governor.

'Woodstock,' he said, 'I'm told you're between the devil and the deep blue sea. Which do you prefer?'

'The devil,' said Harry. 'I can't swim.'

'Hell can be extremely painful,' said the governor.

'I've never met anyone who's been there,' said Harry.

'If someone in your position were told of a way out, do you think he'd take it?'

'Depends who he was, sir,' said Harry, 'and what the way out was.'

'You could be a valuable citizen, if you wanted to be,' said the governor, 'and there are several people who'd be prepared to help you be one.'

'People are very kind,' said Harry.

'It isn't entirely kindness,' said the governor. 'You have information which we badly want, and we're prepared to pay for it. You could go back into the world with a decent job and some money in no time, if you'd be sensible. I'll tell you, Woodstock, I've never said this to a man before. It's not a governor's job, and I don't like doing it now. But, when I see a man like you letting slide an opportunity which might make all the difference to you for the rest of your life, I'd feel awkward if I hadn't at least taken some steps to try and help you.'

'It's very good of you, sir,' said Harry.

'But people who want help have got to help themselves a bit,' said the governor.

'I haven't said I wanted help, sir,' said Harry.

'I know you haven't, but everybody wants help. There's nobody in such a good position, or such a strong position, or such a happy position that they couldn't do with some help. And of course the worse the position you're in, the more you need it.'

'Surely, sir,' said Harry, 'it depends who you are. You as a governor in this prison may need help, sir. But I as one of your prisoners do not.'

'That's all nonsense,' said the governor, 'and you know it. It's just pride or stupidity, or a mixture of both.'

'I don't know why you think I could give you information

about Stephen Stratford, sir,' said Harry. 'Everyone seems to think I can. But I haven't the faintest idea where he is.'

'If you had, would you tell me?' said the governor.

'I doubt it,' said Harry, 'but it depends on all the circumstances. I never did much care for hypothetical questions, sir.'

'Canon Abdale gives you a very good character,' said the governor.

'That's more than they do when I come up for sentence,' said Harry.

'I can't understand why you never try to go straight. Life's much easier that way.'

'Would you know, sir?' said Harry. 'You've never tried the other way.'

'That's true,' said the governor. 'But I've seen the inside of a prison often enough.'

'But only from the right side of the cell door,' said Harry. 'If I may say so, sir, you can't possibly tell what it's like to be locked up, because you never have been locked up. You get a chance of thinking when you're in prison which you never have outside. Think of the responsibility you've got. I don't simply mean you, sir, but think of the responsibility everybody outside prison has. We've none inside – just a few simple rules to comply with, and the rest of the time's our own. You can really get to grips with yourself. But it takes a long time, sir.'

'Is that why you come back so often?' said the governor. 'In order to get to know yourself?'

'I can't say that it is,' said Harry. 'But I must admit that I don't like responsibility. An honest man has got to be responsible. A dishonest man needn't be.'

'Have you no pride at all?' asked the governor.

'As much as most people, I should think,' said Harry. 'But has pride anything to do with it, sir? I should think a safebreaker is just as proud of a neat job done quickly as another type of engineer is in a legitimate trade.'

'But would you get no pleasure from being able to walk along the street saying to yourself, "I'm a free man. I needn't be frightened of the next policeman I meet. I needn't be worried when I hear a knock on the door"?'

'Policemen and knocks on the door don't worry me, sir. It's all part of my life.'

'But why?' said the governor. 'In heaven's name, why?'

'You should ask Canon Abdale that, sir,' sad Harry. 'He knows more about Heaven than I do. Well, I suppose laziness is at the bottom of it. Most criminals are lazy and I'm no exception. It's easier not to comply with the rules.'

'Well,' said the governor, 'at least I have tried to help, and if you change your mind, say you want to see me.'

'I'm most grateful, sir,' said Harry, and he was taken back to his cell.

17 *The Pay-Off*

A few days after his release Harry paid an unexpected call on the colonel. He had with him the £20,000, which he always collected immediately on being released in case he should meet Stratford. It was indeed like the mythical sop which the Greeks supposed dead people to carry on their journey to Hades for the purpose of quietening the dog which stood guard at the gates.

The colonel was in his flat having a cup of tea with his cousin when they heard the door open and shut again quickly. He went to the door at once and arrived to see Harry bolting the door from the inside.

'My dear boy,' he said. 'How good to see you. But what on earth are you doing?'

'I'm terribly sorry, sir,' said Harry. 'I hoped you wouldn't be here.'

'What are you talking about?'

'I'm afraid I'm in a bit of a mess,' said Harry. 'And now I've landed you in it too.'

'That will be a pleasant change,' said the colonel. 'We're in it together again.'

'That's truer than you think, sir,' said Harry. 'I hope there's nobody else here.'

'I'm afraid there is,' said the colonel. 'My cousin, Lady Mary.'

'Oh good gracious,' said Harry. 'Well, I'll have to tell you about it. There's a man following me who's trying to murder me.'

'Well, that's simple enough,' said the colonel. 'I'll get on to the police.'

'That would be simple enough,' said Harry. 'But you can't, I'm afraid, colonel.'

'Have they cut the lines already?'

'It isn't that,' said Harry. 'You remember, sir, I told you that I did a certain amount of Secret Service work?'

'Yes, indeed,' said the colonel.

'Well, this is a bit of it. The police mustn't under any circumstances be brought into it.'

'But I'm not going to let anybody murder you in cold blood,' said the colonel. 'You saved my life. Perhaps I can save yours this time.'

'I'm afraid it may come to that,' said Harry, 'but I'm worried about Lady Mary.'

'She's got guts,' said the colonel. 'Should have been a man really.'

'I dare say,' said Harry, 'but I don't like ladies about the place when the shooting begins. Mark you, I don't like the shooting to begin anyway.'

'Well, you must come in. You've bolted the door. You can't do any more. And we'd better tell Mary. She'll understand.'

They went back to the sitting-room where Lady Mary was eating her sandwiches. They had not been made by the colonel. She had bought them from Fortnum and Mason.

'What a delightful surprise, Mary. I was only talking about him the other day, and here he is.'

'How do you do?' said Lady Mary. 'How nice to meet you at last.'

'I'm not sure you'll think so in a moment, ma'am,' said Harry.

'Are you going to wolf all my sandwiches, then?'

'Mary,' said the colonel, 'I'm afraid this is serious.'

'Well, wait till I've finished my sandwiches and tea,' said Lady Mary.

'I'm afraid it can't wait,' said the colonel.

'Oh, well,' said Lady Mary. 'Tell me what it is. Has there been a revolution or something?' She started to eat another sandwich. 'I certainly intend to finish these before it comes to us. Why shouldn't people revolt if they don't like what's good for them? I never liked what was good for me. I often revolted. Is it students, or anti-something people, or what?'

'It's only anti-me, I'm afraid,' said Harry.

'Why should anybody be anti-you?' said Lady Mary. 'For saving George's life? You might have done better, I agree, but you could have done a good deal worse. He's kind and fairly clean about the house. And his rudeness is more entertainment than anything else.'

'Mary, this is really serious,' said the colonel. 'A man is on his way to try to murder Mr Woodstock.'

'Not in the 1960's in Albany, surely?' said Lady Mary.

'I'm afraid so,' said Harry.

'Well, it makes a change,' said Lady Mary.

'It'll make a considerable change to me,' said Harry, 'if he succeeds.'

'That's a point,' said Lady Mary. 'Do you think he will? He'll have a good chance, I'm afraid. How soon will he be here?'

'Very soon, I should think. He's just out in Piccadilly now.'

'Well, I'm afraid I'm not going to stand in front of you and say: "Shoot, if you must, this old grey head, but spare Mr Woodstock". I'm not cut out that way. What are the police doing?'

'We can't bring them into it,' said the colonel. 'It's a Secret Service matter. And the vital interests of the country may be at stake.'

'How aggravating,' said Lady Mary. 'I've never dialled 999. This would have been a glorious opportunity. We'll have to do it if they murder you, why not before? Do the Secret Service want you murdered?'

'You don't understand these things,' said the colonel. 'And you mustn't ask Mr Woodstock any questions about it. His lips are sealed.'

'The whole lot of you will be sealed in a moment, from what you say, if you don't do something about it,' said Lady Mary. 'I must say, it's quite a nasty thought to see you standing up there in the full flush of life – I said life, not youth – and to think that a few minutes later you may just be a corpse.'

'There's no need to rub it in,' said the colonel. 'Besides, if it comes to that, we may all be corpses. He may shoot the lot of us.'

'Well, I'm not in the Secret Service,' said Lady Mary. 'Why shouldn't I ring the police?'

'Because you mustn't,' said the colonel. 'The country comes first.'

'I'm so very sorry about it,' Harry said. 'I thought I'd evaded him when I slipped in here, but to my horror, as I came in, I saw that he'd spotted me.'

At that moment, there was a knock on the door.

'Do you know,' said Lady Mary, 'if I were standing up, I should sit down, or I might fall down. I feel quite faint. Are you going to answer it?'

The colonel and Harry exchanged glances. Harry then went out of the room to the front door.

'Who is it?' he said.

'Me,' said Sonia.

'Oh, good lord,' said Harry. 'Go away, go a long way away.'

'I'm not going,' said Sonia. 'And Canon Abdale is with me.'

'Hell,' said Harry.

'Come on, Harry,' said the canon, 'let us in.'

Harry withdrew the bolt, opened the door, let them in and shut it again quickly, and bolted it.

'What on earth do you want to come here for?' he said to Sonia.

'I wanted to see you,' said Sonia. 'I couldn't find you. So I went to see Canon Abdale. He suggested Colonel Brookside might know where you were. So here we are.'

'Well, take a good look at me,' said Harry. 'This may be the last time.'

'What on earth do you mean?' said Sonia.

'I'll tell you in confidence,' said Harry.

'What is it?' said the canon.

'He's after me and knows I'm here.'

'I shall get on to the police,' said the canon.

'No,' said Harry, 'you won't. I told you in confidence. And you're not to break it. This is my business.'

'It's ours now,' said the canon.

'You shouldn't have come here.'

'What do you propose to do?' said the canon.

'Wait and see,' said Harry. 'I've got something to give him. Perhaps he'll take that and buzz off, when he sees how many witnesses there are.'

'Aren't you alone?' said the canon.

'No, the colonel and his cousin are here. Come in.'

They all went into the sitting-room.

'Now there are three of us,' said the colonel. 'We ought to be able to deal with one man.'

'Five,' said Lady Mary.

'Well, what's the plan?' said the colonel. 'You're in command, you know, not me. What's the object?'

'The object,' said Harry, 'is to get rid of him as cheaply as possible, and without involving the police. I've got something in that bag which may interest him.'

'Out-of-date plans, I suppose,' said the colonel. 'Things which will do him no good at all.'

'On the contrary,' said Harry. 'The things that I've got in that bag will do him a lot of good.'

'I'm not going to guess,' said the colonel. 'What I know quite well is that you wouldn't give away anything of value.'

'Well, you're wrong, sir,' said Harry. 'I'm proposing to give away something of considerable value.'

'Vital to the country?' said the colonel incredulously.

'Not particularly,' said Harry, 'but valuable to me.'

'Ah, that's different,' said the colonel. 'May I ask what it is?'

'Certainly,' said Harry. 'It's money.'

'You can bribe these chaps, then?'

'Some of them,' said Harry. 'One thing I can tell you for certain. This chap will take the money.'

'So you offer him that to leave you alone? Might I know how much it is?'

'About twenty thousand pounds,' said Harry.

'Good gracious,' said the colonel. 'Do you carry that around with you?'

'Sometimes I have to in my business,' said Harry. He looked at the canon. 'Did you want to say something, canon?' he asked.

'No, thank you,' said the canon. 'Not at the moment. I was just listening.'

'While we're waiting,' said Lady Mary, 'suppose we play a word game? I'll begin. "A".'

'Might I know what the rules are?' said the canon.

'Three lives each,' said Lady Mary. 'Words of four letters don't count. Your go next, canon.'

'Forgive me,' said the canon, 'might I know a little more? What's the object of the game?'

'Not to end a word. You lose a life if you end a word. You can cheat if you like, but if you're challenged and haven't got a good answer, you lose a life. If you're challenged and you have got a good answer, then the person who challenges you loses a life.'

'I think I remember,' said the canon. 'I'll say "B".'

' "A",' said the colonel.

' "C",' said Sonia.

'That's rather hard on me, isn't it?' said Harry. 'I would have thought that in the circumstances you'd have given me something a bit more helpful. I can only think of one word.'

'There is another,' said the canon.

At that moment, there was a ring at the bell.

'I'll go,' said Harry.

He went out of the room and straight to the door, unbolted and opened it. It was Stratford.

'Come in,' said Harry. 'I've been expecting you. This way.'

He led Stratford into the sitting-room.

'I won't trouble to introduce you,' he said.

'Where is it?' said Stratford.

Harry said nothing, but handed him the bag, and then walked to the other end of the room. Stratford opened the bag and found the notes in it.

'How much is there?' he asked.

'Twenty thousand,' said Harry.

Stratford examined the notes and made a quick calculation to see whether that sounded reasonable.

'Where's the rest?' he asked.

'Evaporated,' said Harry. 'It slipped through my fingers. I couldn't hold it.'

'You bastard,' said Stratford.

'Quite,' said Harry. 'But twenty thousand is a good deal better than nothing. You didn't think you'd find anything.'

Stratford stepped backwards towards the door of the sitting-room.

'No doubt, you think it very funny,' said Stratford. 'But I don't, and perhaps this will change your mind about it.'

He pulled out a revolver, fired one shot. Harry put his hands in the region of his heart and slumped to the ground.

'Well, laugh that off,' said Stratford, and rushed out of the room to the front door, while the others went towards Harry. As soon as the front door had slammed, Harry got up.

'It's not easy to hit anyone with a revolver,' he said. 'But I didn't want him to try twice. I'm afraid he made a nasty hole in that chair.'

Sonia rushed to Harry and kissed him.

'Now, there's no time to be lost,' said Harry. 'When he finds out I'm all right, he'll be after me again. There's nothing for it.' He looked round the room and saw on the colonel's desk his gold fountain pen. He picked it up, went to the telephone, and dialled 999. He asked for the police, and when he was put through, he said he was speaking for the colonel.

'A man has just stolen Colonel Brookside's gold fountain pen. He's got him at his flat in Albany at the moment, but he can't guarantee to keep him, so will you send round some officers at once.' Harry replaced the receiver.

'What *is* all this?' said the colonel. Harry drew him on one side.

'It's got to be done this way, I'm afraid, sir,' he said quietly. 'It's the only way. Please don't make it difficult for me.'

'What do you want me to do?' asked the colonel.

'Just identify your pen and say that I took it.'

'But they'll arrest you.'

'Exactly,' said Harry. 'I shall be quite safe where they take me.'

'But I don't want to charge you with stealing. You haven't stolen it, anyway.'

'I have,' said Harry. 'Look, I've got it and I won't give it back to you.'

The colonel looked puzzled.

'Now do help me, sir,' said Harry. 'It's the only way.'

'Well, if you really mean it,' said the colonel. 'You did much more for me. In fact, it looks like biting the hand that fed me to charge you with stealing. But if that's what you want, I'll do it.'

An hour later Harry was safely in custody, and three weeks later he was back in prison.

When the time was drawing near for his release, Harry learned that Stratford was back in England, and he knew why. He immediately started to break some of the prison rules in order to lose his remission. A few days later the canon called on him.

'Good news, Harry,' he said as soon as the prison officer had left them alone together. Once again Harry regretfully knocked him down. A mug was knocked on to the floor in the process.

'You bloody fool,' said the canon, still lying on the ground nursing his chin. 'I wanted to tell you they'd caught Stratford.'

At that moment the prison officer returned.

'What's all this?' he said.

'Just a slight accident,' said Harry.

'An accident, eh?' said the prison officer in obvious disbelief. 'Did he strike you, sir?'

Many thoughts raced through the canon's head. He felt almost certain that, if Harry came out from prison in the next few days he would get married to Sonia, and that there was an extremely good chance that he would go straight in the future. He had given up the twenty thousand pounds, so he would not even be starting with stolen money. The canon had been working on Harry for years and his reformation had been one of his greatest ambitions. If Harry served a further six months in prison now, anything might happen during that period. He himself might die. Sonia might be knocked down in the street and killed. He felt that it was now or very likely never.

Although in the split second, which was all he had in which to make a decision, he could not be completely sure that his object was Harry's welfare rather than his own satisfaction in reforming him, he honestly believed that it was love and not pride which dictated his answer. He got up.

'It was an accident,' he said. 'A mistake – call it what you will. There's no charge to be made.'

'I'm afraid you must leave that to me, sir,' said the prison officer.

'It was nothing,' said the canon.

'If this matter goes before the visiting justices,' said the prison officer, 'are you prepared to say that the prisoner did not knock you down?'

Once again the thoughts, which had raced through the canon's mind a few seconds before, did the lap in record time.

'Yes,' said the canon.

'Very well,' said the prison officer. 'If you say so, sir.' But after he had left the cell, he crossed himself.